FELLING BECHET

STELLA WILLIAMS

SERPENTINE CREATIVE LLC

Copyright © 2022 by Stella Williams

All rights reserved.

No portion of this book may be reproduced in any form without written permission from the publisher or author, except as permitted by U.S. copyright law.

CONTENTS

CONTENT WARNINGS

This book contains themes and content related to sexual assault, verbal abuse by a family member, and mental health issues.

FELLING

fell/fel/
verb

- 1.cut down (a tree):"33 million trees are felled each day"

Source: Oxford Dictionary

CHAPTER ONE

"**N**o peeking!" Jay pulled her hand away from her face.

Isis frowned beneath the blindfold and folded her arms across her chest.

"I don't have time for games, Jay."

"You know, the Queen of Ice could thaw out a bit, especially for her birthday," he said, pushing her forward.

If anyone else called her the Queen of Ice, Isis would tear them a new one. Being her best friend, Jay was receiving a lot of passes this evening, starting with the whole business of being blindfolded. She knew he liked putting together big surprises, and it was her birthday, so she was rolling with it, despite her protests. Besides, Jay was fantastic at surprises. Last year was a deep-sea fishing trip. The year before that, they had gone hiking through the Grand

Canyon. With her line of work, their adventures were the highlights of her year.

This year, however, a big vacation surprise hadn't been possible. A major scandal had hit the mayor's office, and the entirety of the local politics was scrambling to see just how far it reached and who would come out on top. Hardly the time for Isis to disappear, even just for the weekend. So here she was, blindfolded and dressed up for a night out, anxiously awaiting her surprise.

Being in a skintight dress and heels didn't usually signal a good time for her, but that didn't mean she wouldn't like what Jay had planned. Jay blindfolded her once they got in the car, and after a short drive, they had parked, taken an elevator up at least thirteen floors, and were now walking down a quiet carpeted hall. It was unnerving, and she definitely wouldn't be going along with it if she didn't have absolute faith in him. At least, Jay didn't seem to be taking her to a club. Now that *would* be a nightmare.

When they stopped again, Isis reached for her blindfold once more, and when Jay didn't stop her, she tore it off. Her eyes adjusted to the light, and her frown deepened.

"You have got to be shitting me," she said, turning on her heels.

Jay caught her in his arms and turned her back toward the glass doors with the damning sign.

Grand Vista Rooftop Lounge K Hotel

"Come on, Isis! It was high school. Kevin isn't that bad anymore," Jay said.

Isis shook her head.

"Kevin is still an asshole, and regardless whether he's here tonight, you know I don't patronize his ashy behind."

"You aren't. I'm covering everything tonight," Jay said.

Isis glared at him, she knew that Jay and Kevin were frat brothers, but he'd never pushed her in her insistence to not associate with Kevin before. She wondered what the real reason for bringing her here was.

"Fuck that! I'm not subjecting myself to that man—especially not on my birthday."

Jay rolled his eyes.

"I didn't bring you here to mingle with Kevin. Charlotte assured me there is a fair number of educated, melanated men meeting up tonight," Jay said.

Isis looked beyond the glass entrance door and saw Charlotte waving at them from inside. She shook her head and turned her attention back to Jay.

"I don't need help in the romance department."

"Really? So, what happened with Richard?"

Isis rolled her eyes at the mention of her last attempt at dating.

"He never said we were exclusive, and I shouldn't have assumed."

"See, this is what you get for dating those country club, white boys all the time. They date you for a minute until they realize dating a Black woman doesn't go over well with their racist ass circles."

"It's not my fault they seem like the only ones interested," she muttered.

Jay put his hands on her shoulders and made her look into his eyes.

"Trust me, they aren't. You just don't take Black men seriously, and it's a damn shame."

Offended, Isis pushed away from him.

"That is not true. I have gone on dates with lots of Black men. None of them have ever wanted to continue past a date or two."

"Look, you are my best friend. My A1, day 1. My cradle to the grave. I have to be honest with you. You always, whether on purpose or not, always sabotage the fuck out of a relationship. Starting with dating men you know damn well don't take you seriously. Ending with all the good brothers you pass over because they don't fit that little narrow ass box you constructed of who your perfect soulmate should be," Jay said.

"So having standards is a crime?"

"No, but ever since West spread that rumor that he took your V under the bleachers in middle school, you have been hypercritical of any man you're attracted to," he said.

"Seriously, that was middle school," Isis said, and he chuckled.

"But the memory still gets to you. Just like whatever Kevin did to get under your skin in high school. You hold a grudge like nobody's business, Isis. Don't you think now is a good time to let that bullshit go and try something new? It's not healthy," Jay laughed.

Isis wanted to protest more, but she didn't want to let one man ruin what could still be a fun night.

"Fine, I guess since I'm already here," Isis said.

Jay smiled and opened the door for her. She stepped through into the swanky outdoor space.

"Happy Birthday, Isis!"

Charlotte gave her a hug and shoved a drink into her hand. It was a frothy pink concoction that was sure to be the death of Isis's inhibitions, but she smiled anyway and took a sip. Sweet, fruity deception, that's what it was. Not a hint of alcohol, except her head was already feeling lighter and her limbs looser.

"Thank you," Isis said.

Jay looped his arm protectively around Charlotte's waist and placed a kiss on her cheek. He whispered something into Charlotte's ear that made the woman giggle. She whispered something back that had Jay biting his lip and looking like he wanted to devour her then and there. Seeing them so cutesy and in love filled Isis with warmth and longing. She wanted what they had, but if her experiences with dating were any indication, maybe she just wasn't made for that kind of all-consuming emotion.

With the couple occupied, Isis found a spot to discard the dangerous concoction Charlotte had given her and made her way to the bar to get something more her speed. She had just gotten the bartender's attention when a man a good two inches shorter than she was leaned on the bar next to her. Isis had nothing against short men, but the way he leered at her, licking his lips, was already a significant turnoff. She ordered her drink and did her best not to make eye contact. Even if she vowed at that moment to be more receptive to someone outside of her usual type, he most definitely wasn't it.

"I got this one if you slide with me out on the dance floor," the man quipped.

Isis bit the inside of her cheek to keep from making a face. Instead, she kept her eyes trained on the line of alcohol backlit on the bar. The music was loud enough that she could believably pretend not to hear his tragic attempt at picking her up. The bartender came back with her drink, and the man slid his card across the bar.

The bartender looked at Isis with a raised eyebrow, and she shook her head.

"Tab under Jay Thompson, thank you," Isis said pleasantly.

The man snatched his card back before scowling at her.

"You coulda just said you had a man already," he spat and stormed off.

Isis rolled her eyes and scanned the rest of the crowd as she sipped her whiskey and ginger soda. Former company excluded, Isis had to admit there were plenty of good-looking men in the crowd. Tall, short, light-skinned, dark-skinned, some in slacks and others in dark jeans. The crowd was a decent mix of the Black male diaspora. It wasn't until Isis noticed that several men had visible scarring in roughly the same shape—a brand, to be more exact. She frowned, taking a closer look at the room.

Tonight's buffet of men wasn't a coincidence. It was a fucking Frat party. The very Fraternity Jay belonged to. Her suspicions were confirmed when she saw Dominic Westmoore and Kevin Kerrigan waltz into the club. If she had been pissed before, it was nothing compared to how she felt now. This night wasn't about her. Jay lied about why he'd brought her here. It was about him keeping appearances. She downed her drink and made her way slowly towards the door, trying to not be noticed by Kevin.

Unfortunately, the man was like a heat-seeking missile when it came to sniffing her out at social events. In her attempt to slide around the massive linebacker-built man that was currently impeding her escape, she ended up bumping right into Kevin. He was surrounded by women and wore all black, as was his M.O. Dark colors to suit the darkness of his soul. He glared at Isis before a devious smile tipped his thick, lipstick-stained lips.

"Well, well, well! If it isn't the Queen of Ice," he laughed.

She froze, her fists balling up until her nails dug painfully into her palms. It didn't matter that she was a fully functioning adult. Being around Kevin always made Isis feel like an insecure teenager all over again. Isis shuddered just thinking about the incident that cemented her distaste for Kevin Kerrigan. Him sliding into the seat next to hers at lunch. That smarmy smile of his as he slid his hand along her arm before placing her hand on the bulge of his pants.

"See what you do to me, Isis?"

She tried to pull her hand away, but his grip was too firm. He forced her hand over the bulge, a satisfied sigh escaping his lips just before she closed her fist around him as tight as she could and twisted.

"You're a fucking creep, Kevin. Stay the hell away from me!"

Her enraged shout echoed through the courtyard just as Kevin's friends rounded the corner. They all stared for a moment, trying to figure out the scene before them. Isis stormed away from Kevin, and at the last moment, before she was out of earshot, he yelled back at her.

"You're a frigid bitch, Isis! A god-damned Queen of Ice!"

It was high school, and he was rich and good-looking. Teenage girls and teachers alike had fallen at his feet to do his bidding. Not Isis. She didn't have time for boys back then and refused to make time for them now.

That didn't stop the nickname from finding a home right in the middle of her self-confidence. Kevin knew it too. He shot her a gotcha grin and moved along, dragging his little entourage with him.

Isis rolled her eyes and marched over to the elevators that would take her downstairs and away from the possibility of further humiliation by the man. Luckily the elevator was there, so she didn't have to wait and further be humiliated. As the elevator door slid closed, sealing Isis away from the party and leaving her alone with her thoughts, she let her guard fall just for a moment. Isis didn't want to admit that maybe Jay was right. She was holding onto a grudge from high school. She hadn't told anyone at the time what happened, not even Jay. She'd shoved it down with the rest of her trash experiences at the hands of men. Her interactions with Kevin now was another story entirely. It wasn't so much a specific thing that Kevin did to get under her skin. Everything about the man rubbed her the wrong way. Whether it had anything to do with the incident in high school or not, Isis knew for a fact she wasn't the only one who took issue with Kevin.

Whether she turned a new leaf tonight or not, anything to do with Kevin was a no-go for her. Isis was so caught up in her stewing she didn't notice the elevator had only gone down a single floor before she got off. She found herself being greeted by an entirely different party than the one upstairs. The hall was lit only by candles, and a man in a suit quickly approached her and handed her a black silk mask.

"This way, miss," he said.

Isis turned to see the elevator door already closed and heading down. Turning back to the man, he looked at her expectantly. She peered beyond him in the direction of the soft classical music and caught a glimpse of men in all black suits and women in little black dresses twirling around in a grand dance. It was something out of a classic movie if you ignored the modern dress of everyone. She could easily tell the man she was in the wrong place, but her curiosity won out. She put on the mask, glancing back at her reflection in the steel of the elevator. She felt like an extra in a movie. Her little black dress and strappy heels seemed like the uniform of the evening. No wonder the man assumed she was meant to be there.

With her disguise in place, she was led down the hall to the entrance of what appeared to be a grand ballroom. It had polished ebony floors and floor-to-ceiling windows that made it seem like they were dancing on the stars above the city skyline. It was breathtaking.

She made her way to the window, grabbing a glass of champagne from a passing waiter. Now, this was how she could spend her birthday. Sipping champagne and admiring the gorgeous view in front of her. Isis had never seen the city like this before. Mostly because she was often too busy with her work to enjoy the view. From this high, the hustle and bustle of the streets below only existed as a million dancing lights. Her posture relaxed as the euphoric combination of the view and bubbly champagne worked their magic. The tension from her confrontation with Kevin slipped away and for the first time in months, Isis felt entirely at ease.

Bechet Cross twirled his dance partner one last time before bowing out of the next dance. She had been lovely to chat with and had been his first choice of the evening until he'd seen *her*. The latecomer had caught the eye of a few people in the room. The men and women all dressed the same at these events, and the uniform was required to aid in the anonymity of it all. Bechet had been attending Kevin's private socials for a few months now, but this was the first he'd seen of her. She stood out amongst the homogeneous sea like a tide bringing along fresh nutrients to his parched shores.

She ignored the attention of others as she made her way to the windows. Her eyes sparkling and a slight smile created a cute little dimple on her cheek. She was elegant and mysterious, and he had to get to know her. Bechet's dance partner looped her arm in his, no doubt expecting to be escorted to one of the private rooms down the hall. Bechet smoothly removed her hand from his arm and kissed the tops of her knuckles.

"My apologies, I will not be keeping your company this evening," he said coolly.

The woman pouted slightly before moving away from him. Another reason Bechet enjoyed this sort of thing. No one was genuinely bothered by rejection; it was made clear that not every evening would end with carnal pleasures. This was more of a social club than anything. A chance to mingle and enjoy oneself without the pressures and expectations of one's reputation.

Private rooms were used for card games and deep conversations just as often as for sex and other debaucheries. Bechet grabbed a glass of champagne from a passing waiter and made his way to a wall of windows. He didn't approach her right away. He wanted to study her for a bit, determine what her motives were for being here.

Most of the members were prominent business people, not so many athletes or musicians, but definitely the powers and money behind them. That didn't mean there weren't a few escorts scattered among them. Bechet doubted she was an escort, though. They usually scanned the room for clients, not ignore everyone for a view that most of the members routinely saw from their own penthouses and corner offices.

She continued to stare out the window, even as men and women alike approached and tried to get her attention in subtle ways. She would acknowledge them briefly with a nod but didn't speak. He yearned to hear her voice, to see if it had rich undertones like her chestnut skin or if it was soft and silky like the satin fabric of her dress. This woman intrigued him, and he hadn't been intrigued by anyone in a long time.

After almost ten minutes, Bechet knew he needed to make a move. She was starting to shift her weight, probably to ease the tension in her calves from standing in the thin-strapped heels she wore. It only heightened his desire as her hips swung with each movement, inching her dress slowly up her thighs. An erotic peep show. The flash of a red lace could be seen for anyone paying close enough attention. His fingers itched to travel along the same path and determine if it was a slinky pair of lace boy shorts, or one of those sexy thigh garters that women with thick thighs wore.

He could no longer be patient. She would soon move along, maybe even leave. It was clear she hadn't come here to socialize, which made her even more of an enigma. Before he could get his chance, another man approached her. This man wasn't taking the subtle route like the others. When the woman turned and smiled at the man, Bechet was simultaneously stunned by its radiance, and angry that he hadn't been the one to receive such a look from her. When it seemed they were going to have a chat, a big ball of jealousy settled in his stomach. He'd obviously missed his chance. The urge to fight for this woman's attention was enough to cool Bechet's interest just a little.

The last woman who had garnered this much interest from him was why he preferred these anonymous parties in the first place. Turning back to the room, Bechet was just about to leave himself when the other man turned and moved away from the woman, frowning. Maybe his luck hadn't run out just yet.

Isis continued to grin as the rude man went on his way. Bill, or whatever he said his name was, wouldn't be enticing her into a hotel room tonight. He obviously hadn't noticed her lack of interest in the others who approached her or thought just maybe his inflated ego would be more to her liking. Isis pulled her phone out of the small pocket hidden in the top seam of her dress. She quickly scrolled through texts from Jay, asking where she had disappeared and why wasn't she answering the phone. She had just pressed send on her reply to them when another man approached. He didn't speak to her at first, just stood well within her personal space for a moment before clearing his throat.

"Excuse me, but would you care to dance?"

Isis tucked her phone away and looked at the man. She had to tilt her head almost all the way back, even in heels. He was so tall. Standing this close, his cologne filled her nose with hints of citrus, cedar, and something salty. He smelled refreshingly outdoorsy in comparison to the cloyingly sweet and musky fragrances worn by the other man.

She was so busy inhaling him that she almost forgot that he'd asked her to dance. Isis' feet were killing her. She hadn't planned to be standing so long in these heels, and dancing didn't seem at all appealing. She pressed her lips together to keep from smiling at the man and shook her head.

"Sorry, I was just about to call it an evening."

An immediate zing of regret hit her as she turned to leave. That and the sharp bite of her aching feet made her stumble just a bit.

The man caught her. His arm secure around her waist, he lifted her slightly, relieving some of the pressure on her feet.

"Of course, those shoes can't be comfortable. Why don't we move to the lounge and chat?"

Before she could protest, he was already guiding her out of the room and toward the elevator. She went along with it only because she would get to the elevator much faster and much less painfully with his help. She could bail on him then. What she hadn't planned on was how simply gorgeous the man was, once they both relinquished their masks to the man at the elevator.

It wasn't that she hadn't noticed the high cheekbones and golden whiskey eyes. It was seeing how his thick eyebrows and lashes framed them without the mask and the thickening shadow of his late-night beard. Isis was a sucker for a man with a beard, even if it seemed this man liked to maintain a clean-cut appearance.

You're obviously attracted to the man. Why are you so harsh?

Isis continued to silently chastise herself as they entered the elevator. She expected him to move away once inside, but he kept his arm around her. His hand was respectfully on her waistline but playfully drifted down to the curve of her hip before sliding back up again. Isis did her best not to lean into him as the heat trail of his touch sent electric currents of arousal through her.

"So, what's your name?" Isis asked to cut the silence and the heat growing between their bodies.

The man looked down at her and smiled.

"Are you sure you want to know? I'm pretty sure you plan on bailing on me as soon as we hit the lobby."

Heat warmed her cheeks as she realized she wasn't as poker-faced as she thought. The thought had indeed crossed her mind, but not any longer. It was her birthday, and she thought Jay had a small point about her being more open to letting her libido take charge every now and again.

"Perhaps I would bail on a stranger, but if I know your name...."

"Bechet, and you?"

"Isis."

"Nice to meet you, Isis. Would you care to join me for a drink in the bar, or would you rather we reschedule for another time?" Bechet asked.

Isis laughed.

"What makes you think I'm interested?"

Bechet pulled her flush against his frame. Isis held her breath as his face inched closer until their lips almost touched. She closed her eyes, expecting the feel of his lips against hers, only for them to brush gently across her left cheek as he spoke.

"Because you wouldn't have allowed me this close if you weren't."

He pulled away with a smug grin, and Isis breathed out a frustrated sigh. He was absolutely right. There was no way she would have allowed him this far into her personal space, let alone stay there, without some sort of attraction. Hell, she was even disappointed he hadn't kissed her. Isis had never been this riled up over a man she had just met. Jay must have really touched a nerve with all his talk of "thawing the ice."

The elevator began to slow, signaling that they were fast approaching their destination. Isis needed to make a decision and fast. She looked up to his expectant gaze and shook her head in disbelief. Typically, a man this self-assured would be a turnoff, but Bechet had already broken down her primary defenses.

"One drink," she said just before the elevator doors opened.

Bechet quickly pressed the door closed button and pulled her back against him before pressing his lips to hers. They were firm and insistent, but not in a desperate way. His tongue teased the seam of her lips, and she opened for him, letting his slick tongue slide past her teeth. She melted into him as they engaged in an intimate battle of tongues, his scent overwhelming her sense of smell and contributing to her lack of self-control.

He was intoxicating, dangerous, and sexy as hell. Isis was in way over her head with this one, and she knew it. Thankfully, there were others in need of the elevator, and Bechet at least had the presence of mind to pull away before the small crowd outside got a glimpse at the show.

Bechet took a deep breath, holding it as he guided the beguiling Isis to the hotel bar. He'd already broken so many of his own rules. Bechet wasn't sure he should take up her offer of one drink. He wanted so much more than that. Especially after the passionate way she'd responded to his kiss in the elevator. Still, the easiest way to his ultimate objective would be to indulge the lady.

She didn't seem to know who he was, or maybe just didn't care. It was always a risk to reveal yourself to someone you met at one of Kevin's parties, but Bechet didn't regret his choice yet. Only time would tell if his dick had got him into trouble once again. His family money and connections brought him attention from women of a certain ilk. The money-hungry and the social climbers. He had no interest in being anyone's sugar daddy. When he finally did decide to settle down, it would be with a woman who had her own goals in life that had nothing to do with living up under a man and having endless spa appointments.

Not that he was thinking of settling right now. Nor did he really care what Isis was after, as long as it got her under him in bed. A relationship wasn't anything he wanted, but he had a feeling that if Isis was just as hot for him as he was for her, then maybe they could come to an arrangement.

He guided Isis into the lounge. A live jazz band played in the front of the house, but he wasn't there for the show. There was one open booth left in the back, and he took the opportunity to scoot her into it.

"Trying to get me in a dark corner?"

There was a smile on her face, but her eyes shone with a bit of nervous energy. Bechet slid into the booth next to her and took her lips once again. "Would you rather we put on another show for the crowd?"

Isis shook her head and pulled back.

"A drink and some light conversation are all I am up for tonight."

"I reserve the right to change your mind," Bechet chuckled before signaling to a passing waitress that they were ready to order.

"I'll take a Cambridge gin and tonic," she said.

"Glenlivet 21 Archive, two fingers, neat," he replied.

The waitress nodded and took off to get their order.

"You sure you didn't want something sweeter?" He asked after the waitress brought back their drinks.

Isis rolled her eyes. "The last thing I need is some sugar-laden alcohol bomb to loosen me up around you," she said.

"And why wouldn't you want to be loose?" as soon as he said the words, Bechet knew he had made a mistake in wording. Confirmed by the fire that flashed in her eyes before she raised a questioning eyebrow.

"I mean, I'm not calling you loose. Nor would I like that. I mean, I like a challenge."

Dear God. I'm rambling like an idiot. What the hell is my problem?

Bechet knew what his problem was. Being so close to her, feeling the heat of her body cradled against his, the soft floral scent she wore tickled his nose and made him think of rolling hills and serenity. He didn't know this woman from Adam, but she was already under his skin.

He needed to cut this evening short. He couldn't afford to let another woman get to him like this. Even if she *was* stunningly beautiful and charming. But when Isis started to scoot around to the other side of the booth, he found himself wrapping his arms around her waist to keep her next to him.

"I'm sorry. My words came out wrong. I am not usually this inept with women."

Isis snorted. "No, a man like you would undoubtedly have women falling at his feet."

The tone of her voice told Bechet he had probably passed a point of no return with the lovely Isis. He should just let her go. Go back to the anonymity of the party upstairs and enjoy much less complicated human interaction. Instead, he pulled her close and nuzzled her neck.

She moaned softly, her body pressing closer to his.

At least I'm not the only one caught up in this fog of lust.

He trailed kisses down and across her exposed collarbone before finding his way back to her lips. They met with a clash of lips and tongues.

The gin and tonic she sipped added a bitter undertone to the warm caramel of her mouth. All thoughts of letting the night end at a drink vanished from his brain, which was already formulating a plan on how to get her to agree to get a room.

"Hot damn! I never thought I'd see the day the Queen of Ice melted at a man's touch. Hey Chet, mind if I watch?" Kevin's voice was like a bucket of ice on Isis' libido.

She shoved out of Bechet's grasp.

Bechet sighed before turning an angry glare on Kevin. "How many times do I have to tell you it's Bechet, not Chet?"

Isis looked from Bechet to Kevin, who was lounging on the opposite side of the booth with that sickening grin of his.

"You know this asshole?" The words were out of her mouth before she could stop them.

Where was her self-control? Oh yeah, in the palm of Bechet, or shall we say Chet's hand.

Bechet had the nerve to look confused before she pushed him out of the booth and out of her way.

"Isis, wait!"

She didn't. She wouldn't. She should have just gone home instead of letting her curiosity get the better of her. Her damn curiosity literally just killed the cat. Her cat. Isis had nearly hoped on Bechet's lap to demand they find a room.

That was the last time her wild pussy was going to get the better of her. Isis stormed out of the hotel and slid into the first cab she could get, only to find she wasn't alone.

"Get out," she snapped.

"Listen, I don't know what is up between you and Kevin, but he has nothing to do with me," Bechet said.

"He seemed chummy enough with you," she spat.

"Listen, am I taking you somewhere or not? I can't just sit here all night," The taxi driver asked.

They stared each other down for a moment before answering the taxi driver at once.

"Mulberry Heights."

They looked back at each other.

"Did Kevin tell you where I lived?"

"So, you two are close?"

"Not in this life," Isis muttered.

She turned to slide out of the cab only to find they were already driving.

"Kevin is a business associate, nothing more," Bechet said.

"A business associate who calls you Chet and doesn't think twice about offering to watch you fuck me?"

"We went to college together, so there is some familiarity, but he is not someone I have ever considered a friend. Anyway, I just didn't want you to leave thinking that I was okay with what happened back there."

Isis avoided looking into his eyes. She wasn't sure she could trust her poker face after a potent mix of alcohol combined with her emotional spiraling. She really did have issues when it came to Kevin, and she silently made a mental note to look for a therapist in the morning. For now, all she could do was keep her eyes averted. She had embarrassed herself enough.

Bechet sighed, "Look if my very loose association with Kevin is that big of an issue..." he began.

Her gaze snapped up to his in disbelief that he could think her so shallow, even if that was kind of the case with this situation. "It's not, but that doesn't change the fact that I will be going home alone tonight."

The moment her eyes met his, Isis knew she had made a mistake. Now all she could do was sink in the deep brown pools of his eyes like an idiot. Bechet took her hand in his and brought it to his lips. He brushed a gentle kiss across her knuckles before smiling up at her.

"Give me a chance to make a better impression. Lunch tomorrow."

Isis knew she should say no. That she should pull her hand away and scoot to the far side of the cab. She wasn't used to being so out of control, and the interruption of Kevin was just the shock she needed to put her walls back up. Yet, her walls weren't nearly high enough to block out Bechet's sex appeal.

She found herself leaning in. A soft yes passed her lips just before his tongue. Despite every red flag and alarm bell going off in her head, Isis couldn't think further than the heat building at her core. The feel of Bechet's hands kneading her back and shoulders in a desperate massage as they necked in the back of the taxi. The fire between them was blazing out of control, and Isis knew she was in way over her head.

Every nerve ending in Bechet's body was on fire. He didn't know what it was about Isis, but there was no way he would let her slip through his fingers because of a simple misunderstanding. Her whispered yes was like a siren's call to his libido. Her soft lips beckoned him, her warm mouth greeting his tongue like an old friend.

Pulling her closer, Bechet's hands had a mind of their own. Rubbing and squeezing like they wanted to memorize every inch. He couldn't get enough of her soft skin and wished like hell they were in a hotel room so he could see her caramel curves in all their glory, instead of just groping her like an animal in the back of a cab.

He only vaguely registered the slowing of the cab and had to force himself to pull away. Isis whimpered softly, her eyes still closed. Her ample bosom heaving like she'd just run a 5k. She looked delicious in the dim light. He pulled out his wallet, tossing a handful of bills at the driver before helping himself and Isis out of the cab.

"You sure you want to sleep alone tonight?" He brushed his hand across her bare shoulder.

Isis pressed her body into his, her tiny hands sliding up his chest. She looked up at him, brown eyes swirling with desire, and nodded.

"Café Yarrow 12:30," she breathed before planting a soft kiss on his cheek, "Goodnight, Bechet."

He watched with bated breath as she walked away from him. The swing of her hips mesmerized him for a moment before he realized he was losing his chance to show her he was truly a gentleman. He had to lightly jog to catch up to her before slipping his arm around her waist.

"At least let me walk you to your building," he said.

Bechet fully expected Isis to protest, but instead, she sank into his embrace.

"To my building, and that is it," she said, stifling a yawn.

A block away, it quickly became apparent that Isis had basically fallen asleep. Bechet tried not to focus on how quickly she'd shifted from seductive siren to sleeping beauty and more on the fact that she was comfortable enough to be half snoring in his arms as they walked. He wasn't entirely sure Isis was aware of where she was going until she stopped under the green canopy of the Mulberry Lofts. He shouldn't be surprised that she lived in such an upscale building, given where they'd met. Still, it came as a shock, considering how she'd stared with awe at the night skyline earlier.

Bechet had toured the Lofts when he'd been searching for a new place in the area and knew that everyone had an equally stunning if not better view of the city. His only guess was that either she was just as much a workaholic as he was and barely had time to enjoy the said view, or maybe she just enjoyed seeing the alternate view from the other side of town. Either scenario made her that much more appealing. He could appreciate a woman who enjoyed the small things.

Isis attempted to remove herself from his arms, but Bechet wouldn't let her go.

"You're sleepwalking. Let me make sure you get to your door."

She turned her smiling face toward his, lids hanging low over her eyes. She looked adorable and innocent before her eyes fluttered open, and she pressed a hot kiss to the side of his neck. He hissed, standing stiffly to keep himself from overstepping the obvious boundary. Bechet hated that she could switch from looking innocent sexy and siren sexy at the drop of a hat.

"Nice try, Romeo. I'm a little tired, but I've got it from here."

She pushed away with more strength than he realized anyone could muster when half asleep and slipped away into the building, her stride purposeful and not the least bit lethargic. Bechet had the sense that he had just been played but couldn't for the life of him think of that in a negative light.

CHAPTER TWO

I sis woke to her phone buzzing incessantly. Her head and feet were killing her, and she had a sneaking suspicion the whiskey-eyed Adonis she dreamed of wasn't just a figment of her imagination.

She slapped at her phone before swiping it off the side table and holding it way too close to her squinting face. At least she'd remembered to take her contacts out before falling into bed. Isis hadn't been drunk, but she was learning that sometimes even light drinking could cause her trouble in the morning as she got older. This time she could blame the overly sweet champagne she had sipped at that weird party.

On her phone were a million texts, mainly from Jay bugging her about last night and a few others from people wishing her a happy birthday, but the message that caught her attention was from an unknown number.

Unknown: I can't wait to see you at lunch, Café Yarrow at 12:30.

Her mind conjured Bechet's smoldering gaze from last night, and her insides melted.

Fuck!

Now really wasn't the time for her to be lusting after any man. Last night had been a revelation of sorts. Jay's words had hit a bit closer to home than she would have liked, and her interactions with Kevin had only cemented the fact that she had some issues to work out before she got serious with anyone. Not that she could say she'd been serious with anyone in the recent past. Richard, for one. He'd been an excellent connection to have for political reasons. The fact that the magic of that man's tongue had extended beyond the political arena had made her lose sight of what truly was going on around her.

Was she pissed he had broken things off? No. Was she pissed by how far back her relationship with him had set her in her career?

Isis didn't really want to think about the answer to that question. Instead, she rolled out of bed and headed to her bathroom. If she was going to be presentable for her hot date, she would need all the prep time she could get. Besides, it would probably be her last for quite a while, and she wanted to leave the dating arena with a bang instead of a pitiful fizzle of complicated emotions. Her phone buzzed again. Another text from Jay asking her to drop off a package he'd had sent to her place.

She rolled her eyes, wondering what expensive nonsense Jay had ordered that he couldn't have Charlotte knowing about.

I: What is this nonsense about a package? Especially after last night.

J: Look, I get I may have overstepped, but don't think I'm just going to let it slide that you went MIA ALL NIGHT.

I: Like I said, stay out of my love life—especially when you can't even get your own damn mail because of your girlfriend.

J: So it was a love connection last night, and you are still a hater.

I: Boy, you want your package or not? Right now, it's about to be returned to sender.

J: My client just showed up. I can't be on my phone like this. Can you please drop it by the shop today?

I: You're lucky you're my best friend.

Isis was just about to put her phone back on the charger when another text came through. This one was from her friend and stylist, Gregory.

Gregory: Hey doll! I regret I have to bail on Saturday. Something came up at work, and I will be out of town. Hope this doesn't put you in a bind.

"Just my luck," she muttered before replying.

I: Thanks for letting me know.

He was her last option, aside from Jay, and they had an agreement that he was off the list when bringing a date to an event, to avoid confusion. Charlotte had been around long enough to understand, but Isis still hated needing to ask the favor of him. After her break up with Richard, finding a suitable stand-in for the many

fundraisers and galas she attended for work had
been hard. She needed to be in the spotlight,
not worried that her date would get pissed that
she was more interested in networking than
necking in a dark corner or, worse, would use her
connections while treating her as nothing more
than glorified arm candy.

Being a woman in politics, especially a young,
single, minority woman, required balancing
expectations versus reality. Isis had worked hard
for the near-flawless reputation she currently
held, her setback with Richard, notwithstanding.
Of course, she could go alone. There was nothing
wrong with her showing up without a date. But a
date just made things easier. With a date, she was
less likely to be propositioned for non-business
matters, and could more easily approach male
colleagues and potential donors without their
partners being suspicious. Slightly less important
was the need to show that she wasn't just some
husband hunter looking for a rich guy to take
care of her, like Richard and his country club
bros had whispered behind her back for months.

A second glance at her phone told her she only
had three hours to make herself look rested and
glowing for her date with Bechet. There was no
time to waste if she also had to make a stop to
drop off Jay's box. She would leave it for later but
didn't want to risk cutting her date short if things
went well with Bechet.

❧ ⬩ ❧

Hints of vanilla tickled his nose, yet another reminder of the sassy woman he'd met the previous night. If there was one takeaway from the evening, Isis was a hard woman to forget. Taking another sip of his espresso, Bechet stared at the skyline before him, the sun rising over the tops of the buildings. Normally, the view was something he would ignore in favor of the business section of the newspaper or the countless emails in his inbox, but today he saw the view through her eyes. It wasn't as beautiful as the sunrise over the mountains of his hometown, but it was beautiful in its own way. The sun glinting off the panes of glass like a diamond under a jeweler's glass. Bechet would love to see the view with her.

Bechet ran a hand over the almost full beard on his chin. Isis seemed to love rubbing her cheeks against his stubble last night. Maybe she was into beards. Bechet picked up his phone and texted his cousin Dom to see if he had an open spot in his chair that morning. It was a long shot, considering Dom had been partying with his frat brothers last night. Still, if Bechet was going to be keeping the beard, he needed to start maintenance immediately, before it turned into an unruly bush like his grandfather's.

The Cross men were big hairy men of the mountains. How Melinda Westmoore fell for a back-country hick like his father, Wilhelm Cross, was a mystery to everybody, but somehow the debutante and the logger made it work. Bechet was the only man in his family not to fell trees for a living. Something his brothers, Baron and Braxton, loved to tease him about, despite Bechet's work to bring the family business into a less environmentally damaging realm. Sourcing, selling, and specializing in furniture made with reclaimed wood was the way to go. He just needed to finalize the contract with Kevin on being the sole provider for his expanding hotel chain, and his family would be set.

Dom's reply text interrupted Bechet's retreat into work brain. He smiled as he went inside to change into a pair of jeans and a t-shirt. A quick stop at the family barbershop, then home to shower and change for his date with Isis. She may have agreed to a lunch date to avoid the temptation to sleep with him, but Bechet was not above a bit of afternoon delight. Besides, lunch at Café Yarrow would be the perfect time to see if she was someone he could see being okay with the relationship he planned to propose. Nothing romantic, just one of mutual physical and companionable benefit.

Isis paused at the door of Westmoore's, the holy grail of iconic barbershops. Owned and operated by the Westmoore family since the 20s, it was the quintessential Black male hang-out. Women were not encouraged to frequent. It was a male safe space with mostly high-end clientele, now that Mulberry Hill had been gentrified. Isis took a deep breath and pushed open the glass door. A small bell ringing alerting every male in the room to her entrance. She purposely avoided eye contact as she made her way over to Jay. His station was third from the front on the left. He smiled when he saw her before turning back to his client. All conversation had stopped when she entered and didn't look like it would be starting again until she was gone.

Not for the first time, Isis wondered just how much was said in those hallowed walls. How many business deals and political careers had been made or broken? It was fascinating and infuriating. As much as this place was a beacon of hope for the Black community, it was a signifier of the old guard. A little boys' club that excluded women in ways that sat wrong with Isis. Still, she held her head high and made no show of her discomfort at their apparent dislike for her presence. Jay had invited her here, and she would go about her business.

"Where do you want me to put this?" she asked, holding up his package.

"Go ahead and open it for me," he said, and she rolled her eyes.

"What am I, your servant now?"

"Nah, if you were on the payroll, I wouldn't tolerate all that sass from you. My hands are busy, as you see, so if you wouldn't mind."

Like the rest of the barbers, Jay hadn't stopped working on his client when she walked in. Even if she hated his tone, she knew the persona he put on for work. While she didn't like it, Isis understood. Pulling out her key, she slit the tape on the box and opened the flaps.

Inside was a fancy new set of hair clippers, and she fought the urge to roll her eyes again. No wonder he'd had them delivered to her apartment instead of his own. Charlotte would be pissed that he'd ordered such expensive clippers while they were trying to save for a house. Jay, however, considered himself a hair artist and spent his money on whatever equipment he deemed would help bring him to the next level in his passion for carving designs into other men's heads. He'd even majored in art during college for that specific reason.

"Those are sick, dude," the barber next to him said, leaning over to have a look.

Isis set them down on his station and crossed her arms over her chest.

"I did you a favor. Now I need one from you," Isis said, and Jay nodded.

"Yeah, what's up?" he asked.

Isis hesitated. She hadn't been prepared for all the male eyes on her and their interest in her conversation with Jay. She should have been considering she was invading their safe space. Isis also didn't feel comfortable admitting that she had trouble finding a date in the middle of a crowded barbershop of powerful men. Sadly, she had already started, and there was no real way to save face at that moment.

"I need you to go with me to an event this Saturday," she said.

Jay shook his head.

"Why can't you go alone?" he asked.

"Reasons," Isis hedged.

Admitting she was dateless in this crowd was one thing. Admitting she needed a date because she didn't feel like facing her not quite ex-boyfriend alone was another. Thankfully, Jay was neither mean nor an idiot and didn't ask for clarification.

"I'll get details later, but I can't go. Charlotte has my whole weekend planned."

Isis bit her lip to stifle a groan. Just as she opened her mouth to excuse herself, Dom Westmoore spun his chair around, and her eyes connected with Bechet's.

"I believe I am free this Saturday."

Isis' eyes widened in shock. She opened her mouth to speak, but nothing came out. She stood there, mouth flapping like a fish out of water. Bechet smirked, sliding smoothly from the chair before crossing the room to her. She took a deep breath. He smelled of cedar and musk, which was the signature scent of Westmoore's aftershave balm. Which she could attribute to the lustrous shine of his beard. Last night it had been barely a shadow, but now was thick enough to perfectly outline and highlight the sharpness of his jawline. She swallowed hard before finally being able to get a grip on herself and form words.

"You still have to make our lunch date before I'd agree."

Bechet slid his hand around her waist. Leaning close to her ear, he whispered. "With that dress on, I'll be making you my lunch."

Isis' world went topsy turvy, and he led her out of the barbershop with a bright smile. Belatedly, she glanced over her shoulder to see Jay scowling and shaking his head at her. She would have to ask him about that later but apparently was now on a date.

Bechet guided Isis out of Westmoore's and onto the sidewalk just outside. As much as he would love to sweep her off her feet, he wanted to wow her on their first date. His current attire was unacceptable.

"I need to freshen up a bit before our date. Would you care to accompany me back to my place?"

Isis raised a perfectly shaped eyebrow at him and slid out of his grasp.

"Nice try. Go get cleaned up, and I will meet you at the café. Don't be late."

She made a show of checking the slim gold watch on her wrist before heading off in the direction of Café Yarrow. Bechet took a moment to admire the view of her backside. Her yellow sundress highlighted the golden glow of her chocolate skin and did nothing to hide her bountiful curves. The tight bodice accentuated her waist before flowing outwards to caress the curve of her hips and stopping to tease the backs of her thighs as she walked. He smiled as he noted her flat sandals did nothing to hide the musculature of her calves and wondered if it was more a choice of comfort over fashion, even as the jeweled sandals reflected the sunlight as she walked.

A slow whistle brought Bechet back to the present.

"Hot damn, look at that."

Bechet turned to the man standing in the doorway of Westmoore's and staring lustfully after Isis.

"She's taken," Bechet practically growled at the man.

The guy just smirked and nodded. "Good for you, man," the man said before disappearing inside.

When Bechet looked up again, Isis was nearly out of sight. He checked his watch and cursed before heading back inside himself. There was no time for him to make it back to his place, shower, change, and make it to Yarrow on time.

"I hope you don't plan on standing her up?" Jay asked as soon as he saw him.

Bechet shook his head and kept walking. He didn't have time to check the man for his assumption. As it was, they were barely acquaintances. Just another one of his college cohort. "Hey, Dom. Mind if I raid your crash pad?"

Dom shook his head and tossed Bechet the keys to the apartment upstairs. It mainly served as an office for Dom. Still, Bechet knew Dom well enough to know he kept a few changes of clothes and amenities there for when business ran late, or he wanted to rendezvous with someone away from his primary residence. Bechet took the stairs two at a time, thankful that Dom had a similar build and fashion taste. He kept his jeans but swapped his shirt out for a soft blue one that stretched across his pecks like a muscle shirt. It wasn't his usual look, but it would have to do. He gave one last check of his haircut and clothes before heading back out the door.

Isis rechecked her watch, and Bechet wasn't late yet, but he was nowhere in sight with three minutes to spare. She had taken her sweet time making it to the rooftop café, just to not be kept waiting, and yet here she was, scrolling through a list of Black therapists and doing her best not to tap her foot in frustration as the hostess asked for the third time if her party was ready.

Bitch, obviously not.

"I can make a reservation for a later time, or there is a more comfortable waiting area on the lower level," the waitress suggested.

Isis pasted on a smile. "That won't be necessary," she said.

The hostess was new and obviously didn't know Isis was a regular and knew the restaurant policy. A fact made clear when the owner herself came out to see why Isis still hadn't been seated.

"Ms. Hale. I'm sorry for the wait. I can place you at your usual table," Chef Lupin said.

Isis opened her mouth to say something, but her body instantly froze as someone large intruded in on her personal space.

"That sounds great." Bechet's smooth baritone swam over her nerves like a lullaby, relaxing all the tension in her body.

She checked her watch, and Bechet had just barely made it. She smiled and nodded, allowing the owner to guide them to the table tucked along the back wall that provided a bit of privacy and allowed for a fantastic view of the park lake.

"I appreciate punctuality, but you were cutting it close," she said as Bechet made a show of pulling her chair out for her.

"Noted," Bechet said before taking his own seat. His large frame perched comically on the thin but sturdy bamboo chair. Isis bit back a laugh as he shifted around as if testing if the chair would hold him.

"Would you prefer we move to a sturdier booth?" She asked.

"No, this is fine, and I already kept you waiting. Let's not complicate things by changing tables," Bechet said.

"Okay, I'm guessing you haven't been here before. Otherwise, you'd have been aware of the chair situation," Isis said.

"You would be correct. I've heard great things about this place, though, so I'm excited to see if their food is better than their seating choice," he said.

"Their seating is fine, but their food," Isis paused to lick her lips, "is delicious."

"What would you suggest for a newbie like me?" Bechet asked.

Isis leaned forward, aware that the bodice of her dress would dip low and reveal an ample amount of cleavage for his perusal. His eyes followed her movements, but he didn't take the bait. His gaze traveled immediately back to hers.

"What is your usual lunch like?" she purred.

"To be honest, anything I can eat with one hand while doing business with the other. If I'm home, my mother makes sandwiches."

"You live with your mother?" She sat back at that.

Bechet smirked.

"I work with her too," Bechet paused as if waiting for her reaction.

"Excuse me?"

The glint in his eyes told her he was teasing her.

"My entire family, really. Our main headquarters just happens to be part of the family estate, where we each have our own lodgings."

Isis relaxed a little but not completely. It was nice to hear that he was obviously family-oriented, but the whole talk of estates signaled red flags that maybe Bechet would be just like every other man she dated: well off, entitled, and only looking for fun. Then again, she wasn't looking for her soulmate right now, so what did it matter?

"I can't imagine working and living so closely with my family."

Bechet shrugged.

"It's not a lifestyle for everyone, but I love it. Family is important to me. What about you? It doesn't seem like you are very close with your family, or am I wrong to make that assumption?"

Now it was Isis' turn to shrug.

"You are definitely wrong for assuming, but then I already knew you were a bit of an ass."

Bechet chuckled and took her hand in his.

"I am an ass man," he leaned slightly to the side, blatantly checking her out, "and you've got quite a nice one."

Isis pulled her hand away, shaking her head. "I bet Kevin finds that kind of humor hilarious."

Bechet frowned.

"Maybe, but Kevin is the last person on my mind right now."

Isis silently cursed herself. She was totally screwing up this date. She was a politician, and she was supposed to be good with people. Maybe it wasn't her, but him? Bechet was an enigma to her. One minute flirtatious and chivalrous, and the next, just a complete ass. Granted, the asshole's behavior mainly was in reaction to her own piss poor behavior.

The waitress came over to take their orders, breaking the sudden tension between them. Isis took that moment to pull herself together.

She could do this. Bechet wasn't anything she couldn't handle. If she could handle the frivolity and circle-jerking of societal life and the political arena, a mid-level businessman like Bechet should be a piece of cake.

A glance at Bechet over the menu and the cute little furrow of his brow as he scanned the menu turned her insides to mush. She was lying to herself. Isis knew it. Bechet had already thrown her for a loop. Maybe because he was ten times more handsome than she remembered, or the fact that his brilliant smile had nothing on the cute little dimple that popped in his right cheek. Maybe she was overwhelmed by the large expanse of chest and muscles he was throwing all in her face with that tight ass shirt on. Whatever it was, her brain was playing defense while her body was throwing the whole game for a chance to climb the mountain of a man like a gym rope.

"I haven't had a chance to look over the menu. Since you are obviously a regular, why don't you order for me?" Bechet asked.

Isis was taken aback by his offer, even more so when it turned out to be genuine.

"We'll have the Okra Stew and a side of fried plantains." She ordered for the both of them, and he flashed her that sexy ass grin of his.

"That sounds delicious," he said as his eyes once again traveled her body before coming back to her face.

Isis hid behind the menu to disguise her flushed cheeks.

Relax, Isis. It's just a first date with a hot guy. You've done this before.

The mental pep talk did little to calm her nerves, especially when she met his molten gaze after handing off the menu to the waitress.

"So, what is it that you do for a living?" She finally regained her composure enough to speak.

Bechet smiled. "The family business is in the logging industry, but I'm working on turning the whole ship around to focus on reclaimed wood and handmade furniture."

Isis hid her shock by taking a sip of water.

"That is not what I expected," she admitted, and Bechet nodded.

"Yeah, not many Black people in the logging business. I'm half-redneck," he joked, but Isis could tell he wasn't entirely kidding, so she didn't touch the subject.

"Well, it mustn't have been easy pitching that change of course to the family," she said, choosing to focus on the reclaimed wood business as a topic of conversation.

Bechet's eyes and face lit up as he started talking about the first time he'd seen reclaimed wood used in a high-end application. He was totally geeking out about wood and furniture, and it was honestly the most adorable thing Isis had ever seen. She could listen to his excited timber and enthusiastic sighs all day and almost did until he caught himself. Clearing his throat, Bechet sat up straighter and deepened his voice.

"So, what is it that you do, Isis?"

"I'm in politics," Isis said, purposely staying vague. In her past experience, men either weren't interested in the specifics or would proceed to talk her ear off about their political views. She braced herself for the former, but Bechet managed to surprise her.

"What kind of politics? City, State, non-profit activism?"

Isis couldn't help the smile that spread from ear to ear.

"Currently city but definitely on track for more."

"Gorgeous, ambitious, great taste in food. You are definitely single by choice," Bechet laughed.

"Definitely by choice. My career takes priority for me. What about you?"

"Same, which begs the question. What are we doing here?"

She set down her fork and crossed her hands in her lap. This turn in conversation wasn't entirely unexpected, but she was shocked by how forward Bechet seemed.

"I'm not against dating. I just prefer to keep things simple. Relationships come with expectations that I don't have time for right now."

Bechet leaned back and studied her for a moment before taking her hand in his. "Ms. Hale, I think we might just be a match made in heaven."

"How so?"

"I feel the same. If I am not too presumptuous, I'd like to propose a deal of sorts."

Isis knew she should be warier of Bechet, but her curiosity and libido were again siding in his favor. She clenched her thighs together like that would stop the deep throbbing between them.

"What are the terms?"

"Simple, just how you like it. We enjoy each other's company, no strings, no expectations, no labels. Discretion is key. Our agreement can start Saturday with me as your escort at the event, or sooner if you would like to explore physical options."

The mention of physical options had her mind and pulse racing. Isis couldn't help but chuckle in an attempt to hide her body's obvious reaction to his words.

"You're cute, you know that."

Bechet was not expecting that reaction from Isis. A drink in the face or a firm no, but the deep belly laugh and passive response were a significant hit to his ego. He wasn't used to women not jumping at the chance to be with him.

"Cute?" He waited for her to elaborate, but she didn't. Instead, she dug into her food like their conversation had reached an appropriate stopping point.

Bechet shook his head before doing the same. Her choice of food was delicious, and he did prefer a hot meal to a cold one. Once their plates were clear, he paid the check and escorted Isis down the stairs.

"I apologize if I was too forward with you," Bechet said.

Isis shrugged her shoulders. "No apology necessary. I've come to appreciate men who are clear about what they want."

There was something about her tone that told Bechet that this appreciation was a new thing for Isis. Everyone had their skeletons. Bechet sure had his own.

"Well, in case there was any doubting what I meant upstairs, I am attracted to you. I think we could be friends, and I certainly wouldn't mind if you were comfortable extending the benefits of that friendship to the bedroom. The caveat: I don't do relationships, and I don't want my business all in the streets."

Isis nodded her head but didn't say anything more. Bechet's gut twisted at the thought that maybe he'd been too candid this time around. That maybe Isis wasn't as straightforward as she claimed she liked her men to be. Bechet didn't have time for games. He'd been burned too badly in the past to allow himself to take that risk. They were halfway to the first floor when suddenly she stopped and forced him against the wall.

Taken off guard, Bechet nearly jumped out of his socks when she pressed her body into his and pulled his face down to meet hers. Her lip gloss tasted of vanilla and honey, exactly how he remembered. All blood rushed from his head to his dick as a hungry little whimper reached his ears. The gut feeling he had before slowly dissolved into intense heat, burning through all his previous doubts. He slid his hands down her back, grabbing hold of her round ass to press her harder into his erection.

He could have kissed her all day, but the sound of approaching footsteps had her out of his arms before his brain registered the newcomers. Isis was already down the rest of the stairs, looking up at him expectantly.

"Thank you for lunch. I'll be in touch about next Saturday."

He cleared his throat and quickly descended, but she was already out of sight. Shaking his head, Bechet pulled out his phone and texted his family that he wouldn't be home that weekend. He licked his lips, tasting her lip gloss there, and smiled. Isis appreciated timeliness, and Bechet enjoyed a woman with practical sensibilities. Something she obviously had if she wore the same lip gloss for day and evening. It was a refreshing contrast from Bechet's usual female companions, who would literally faint at the thought of wearing anything out of season. Bechet wasn't sure if his surprise at the quality of Isis' companionship was a compliment or a sad commentary on his love life post-Rachel. He made his way back to his apartment. One thing Bechet did know for sure was that Isis Hale was going to be trouble.

"Somebody is having a good day," Hector said, placing a latte and the morning newspaper on Isis' desk.

She smiled up at her favorite campaign volunteer. "Have you seen the polling numbers? Of course, today is a good day," she laughed before taking a sip of her coffee.

Hector shook his head and perched himself on the corner of her desk. "I know you're like all business 24/7, but that smile is not a good numbers smile. Someone has finally moved on from the asshole, Richard," he said.

Isis' smile faltered. It wasn't a secret that she and Richard had been more than just friends, but Hector was right. She did her best to keep her private business out of the office. Even being her favorite volunteer, Hector was either very observant, or she hadn't been nearly as careful about keeping her name out of the office rumor mill as she thought.

"Don't you have some canvassing routes to plan?" she snapped, but her words lacked any real bite.

Hector smiled and eased off of her desk. "Right, I'll get right on it," he said and hightailed it out of her office.

Her office space wasn't so much an office as a closet with enough room for a desk and an outlet for her computer to be plugged in. It was temporary, as were most of her offices in the past. Her local position didn't exactly call for an official office, and her campaign work kept her on the move too much to really care. Speaking of, she double-checked that she had packed her extra pair of socks and sneakers. At her level, she covered a lot of physical ground and went through shoes like crazy. It kept her in shape and in touch with the constituents.

As she sat back up, her phone buzzed. She picked it up, a smile spreading across her face when she saw it was a text from Bechet.

B: I hope you are having a productive day at work.

She frowned at his choice of words before texting back.

I: Productive? Yes. Are you?

B: Not really. I can't seem to get a certain woman in a sexy sundress out of my head long enough to get much work done.

Now, Isis smiled.

I: Oh, maybe you should see someone about that.

B: I plan to. Do you have plans tonight?

Isis hesitated. She didn't have plans, but if she agreed to meet with him, that was treading a little too into date territory. Their lunch date had been just a day ago and she didn't want to come off thirsty.

B: You still there? Did I scare you off already?

I: No, I was just checking my schedule.

B: I guess you are busy then? Maybe we can meet for lunch again instead?

Isis definitely would prefer a lunch date. It would put a set limit on the time they spent together and maybe, just maybe she could avoid letting her attraction to Bechet get the best of her. Yet, Isis wasn't about to reschedule her first appointment with the therapist she'd found. The receptionist had told her appointments were nearly two months out for first-time patients but she'd luckily called just after a cancellation.

I: I am busy for lunch, but I am free after work.

B: Okay, shall I make reservations somewhere?

Isis hesitated again. A second date, a dinner date, a public date. She shook her head to clear out the confusion. This wasn't a date. It only made sense that they should see each other again before Saturday, and she had agreed to be a mutual companion of sorts with the man. Maybe that had been a mistake. She was obviously attracted to Bechet, and despite her own admitted need for a no-strings companion, it appeared she was already getting tangled up in feelings she had no business feeling.

I: Let's keep it simple. Takeout at my place?

B: Sounds good, what time should I arrive?

I: Seven

B: Sounds good. Send me your address, and I'll order for us. See you at seven, Isis.

Isis texted him her address and set her phone down. Her palms were sweaty, and her body tingled. Takeout at her place? What the hell was wrong with her? She hadn't even invited Richard inside her home until after a month of dating. She was doing this whole casual thing all wrong, and she knew it. Taking a deep breath, she decided it was best not to overthink this. Having Bechet over for dinner was just like having Jay over. It wasn't even like she had offered to cook either. She could do this, but for now, she needed to focus on her job. This kind of distraction was precisely the sort of thing that would fuel whatever rumors were circulating about her love life.

As if to confirm her suspicions, she peeked out her open office door. She saw Hector chatting animatedly with Raelle, whom Isis had literally hired for her nose for gossip. The easiest way to stay ahead of scandals was to be the first to know about it, and Raelle had a gift in that regard. Isis picked up the newspaper Hector had brought her, and for the first time since the whispers about the mayor's scandal had started, there was front-page news.

Mayor's mistress tells all!

Shaking her head, Isis dove into the article. It read more like a tabloid piece than actual journalism, but they wouldn't have published such inflammatory filth if it hadn't been thoroughly fact-checked. On top of that, there was no mention of the financial scandal, which meant the mayor's team had probably allowed it to cover up the larger story.

The public would be mildly outraged about the mayor's affair with the sheriff's wife, who was also a city council member. He'd make a public apology with his wife by his side. The sheriff's wife might step down from her position and run the following year. Nothing truly career-damaging for either of them.

The story would run for a month, maybe two, giving the perfect cover for the mayoral team to cover up the real shady business happening in its halls. Isis made a mental note to check with

Raelle to see if her source had any more details about the financial issues. Isis didn't play dirty when it came to politics, but that didn't mean she could ignore all the dirty politics at play. Especially if she planned to get any further up the political ladder, which she did.

With a sigh, Isis slipped out of her heels and pulled on her sneakers. Maybe a little door knocking would help her clear her head so she could get back to business. Plus, it never hurt to remind her constituents of her integrity and transparency when her fellow politicians were doing the exact opposite.

Bechet was still smiling at his phone under the table when Margo cleared her throat.

"Chet, is there something you would like to share with the class?"

Bechet looked up with a scowl despite the blush creeping into his cheeks as he shoved his phone into his pocket.

"You know I don't answer to that anymore," he said.

Margo smirked and shook her head. "Well, you didn't answer when I said your name three times, so I took drastic measures. I can give you space if you want to jack off to your latest conquest's tit pics," she said.

Bechet scowled, ready to tear into his friend for making lude comments about Isis but stopped himself. One, he knew Margo was just teasing him. Two, he knew if he showed any hint that he was, in fact, texting a woman, a woman he felt the need to defend, it would open a whole line of questioning Bechet wouldn't and couldn't answer. So instead, he shrugged and lied.

"Sorry, just a text from Brax. Apparently, Christine is causing trouble again."

Barely a lie, when was Baron's wife ever not causing a stir. Bechet didn't need to elaborate with Margo. She'd been around long enough to know about Christine and her attention-seeking outbursts. Had witnessed a few in person.

"So when are you and Braxton going to have the talk with your older brother about getting a divorce?" Margo said.

"I'm leaving that one to Brax and my parents. What were you saying about the Corinthian?" Bechet's not-so-subtle change in subject had everything to do with Bechet trying to avoid another lecture from Margo about trying to salvage his relationship with his oldest brother.

Margo narrowed her eyes at Bechet before pointing at the colorful sketches in front of him. It was an idea sheet from their interior design team. They were going for a rustic modern theme. Perfect for the type of furniture his company created. Though judging by the level of completion of the documents, the design team should have already had in mind a furniture company.

"They had originally contracted with a major brand, but the owners decided to jump on the support small movement. Cross logging is a major brand in its own right, but the furniture department is new and fits what they are looking for, without the risk of going truly mom and pop," Margo said as if reading his mind.

Bechet nodded.

"Alright, so what were you thinking? Do we have a deadline to make the pitch? Who is our competition?"

"Right now, no competition. I am friends with the design lead, so I got the early scoop. They won't start reaching out to companies until next week, as a term of breaking their contract with the bigger company. I think if we send Hunter to scout some local sites for reclaimed wood while Brax works on the first mocks, we can have several pitches to the design team by the end of the month," she said.

"That's cutting it really close. Brax is having a hard time keeping up with our orders as is, especially with the massive order that K Hotel is asking for," Bechet said.

Margo visibly shuddered at the mention of K Hotel. It wasn't a secret that she and Kevin weren't friends in the least. Hell, if Bechet was honest, he didn't know a single person who was Kevin's friend because they actually enjoyed his company. Even in college, there was just something about the guy that did not sit right with Bechet, and that was saying a lot, given Bechet's homelife. The Cross' were a strange group of people, ranging from reckless rednecks to superstitious conspiracy theorists. It was a wonder the family logging business made it to be as successful as it was.

"Can Baron make space at the factory for some of the larger fabrication?"

Bechet scowled at Margo. She knew he wasn't going to ask Baron for anything. Even if he had the will to do it, Baron wasn't exactly suited to the task.

"He's not working the factory anymore. Finally, graduated to the desk. One step closer to the keys to the castle and whatnot," he muttered, hating how bitter he sounded.

"Then hire more people to help Brax with your current orders that he wasn't specifically commissioned for. That should give him enough time to get this done. Honestly, you should have hired more people months ago. Like I told you before you decided you wanted to deal with the devil." Margo's words were harsh, but her gaze shone with concern.

"Kevin is not the best guy. I admit that, but don't you think calling him the devil is a bit much?"

"Honestly, it's not enough to describe the amount of where's the holy water and sage needed around that guy."

Bechet couldn't help but chuckle at Margo's dramatics.

"Anyway, this deal is with his company. We'd be working with his design team, not him directly," Bechet said.

"I know that's a major deal for the company, but honestly, you don't need Kevin or K Hotel to make a splash in this industry. This Corinthian deal, although much smaller, will have a much greater impact in putting the Cross Furniture line on the map," she said.

"True, but I'm not going to turn down a deal that's basically been gift-wrapped and tossed in my lap. Anyway, thank you for getting this Corinthian lead. If you have any other contacts in the market for custom wood furniture," he started.

Margo sighed and stood.

"Yeah, yeah, you know I've got your back, right? Just a word of advice. Be careful with Kevin. He might be a great hotelier, but he really isn't a man you want to be closely tied to. Besides being a total creep, there is nothing good about the folks he has around him," she said before leaving Bechet's temporary office.

Bechet sighed. He knew exactly what Margo was talking about. Kevin Kerrigan, the face of K Hotel Group, was all hype. A pretty face with an eye for a good deal. The real Kevin? Well, he was a mystery, the dark kind that people keep hidden in locked boxes in attics or drop to the bottom of lakes with bricks. His darkness coated everything he touched, people and places alike. Working with Kevin was a risk, but one Bechet was willing to take if it meant he could finally prove that the family legacy of deforestation wasn't the only way.

With Margo gone, Bechet pulled his phone back out to call Braxton and update him on the Corinthian project.

"Hey, bro! How are things at home?" Bechet said as soon as Braxton answered.

"You know nothing out here ever changes. Mom still fussing about staying on trend like we do that socialite shit out here. Dad, hiding in his office to avoid the fuss, and Baron doing his duty as the oldest Cross, but at least Christine is finally off campus," Braxton said.

"Good, maybe Baron will finally grow the fuck up," Bechet said.

"I know you two don't exactly get along but cut the guy some slack. He lost a kid, and now he's kicking his gold-digging wife to the curb. Baby steps," Braxton said.

"Look, you never got the brunt of his holier than thou, 'I'm the boss' bullshit. Anyway, that's not why I'm calling," Bechet said.

"So, I'm not going to touch that brat bomb you just dropped, little bro, but yeah, you called about the K Hotel deal, right? I got the email, and they obviously don't know we aren't some box store manufacturer. That kind of detail, in those numbers, and with such a short deadline. I mean, I love a challenge, but..." Braxton said.

"Yeah, I'm looking it over now. We'll be hiring some more people to help, but getting the army of competent craftsmen capable of this level of work will be damn near impossible. I'll have to chat with Kevin's team, but we'll all be set if we pull this off. No more Crosses risking their lives and their sanity in the Sowell Gate Mountains."

"As someone who nearly lost his life in these mountains, I appreciate the sentiment but come on, bro. These mountains are in our blood. Crazy animal sightings, freak storms, and all that. It's part of what made us."

"That may be true, but that's not all we have to be. Anyway, I'm sending you another email now with details about another more manageable deal that Margo set up."

"Alright, I'll keep an eye out. When are you coming home? I know Mulberry is a big flashy city and all, but I know you're missing the view from Edgewood," Braxton said.

"I'll be home when I get this deal finalized. That's the only way. The view from home will always be there," Bechet said.

"You don't have to beat me over the head with your save the environment platform. I'm already on board, remember. Just don't be a stranger. The longer you're away from the mountain, the more likely you'll see some stranger change into an animal or something," Braxton chuckled.

"Fuck you, Brax. You act like you didn't see something similar," Bechet said.

"I was loopy from blood loss. I'm lucky that bear didn't decide to make a snack out of me and that the fox who chased it off didn't get a chance to come back before I was found."

"Oh, so you are sticking to the 'it was just a fox chasing a bear' story? First, there are no foxes in the mountains, especially not white ones, and what raging bear gives two shits about a lone fox?"

There was silence on the other line before the dial tone let Bechet know that Braxton had hung up on him. Bechet knew he'd pushed too hard. Braxton had only recently gotten more comfortable with talking about his logging accident. That didn't mean he would ever admit to the crazy animal sighting he'd rambled on about, before losing consciousness that day.

His family was no stranger to weird sightings on the mountain. Stories of shifters and mysterious trail guides were common myths in the area. Bechet had been ten years old when he'd had a weird encounter while hiking in the mountains where he grew up. His brothers had been with him, but neither had seen the old man on the ridge shift from a man to a bear. He'd refused to go back into the woods after that, and his father had forced him on a hunting trip to help him get over the fear of what he'd seen. The trip had backfired, leading to Bechet refusing to follow the Cross male legacy of felling trees on Sowell Gate Mountain.

His brothers, more specifically Baron, had never let him live it down, claiming Bechet had fallen to the Cross family curse. The one that made half the family nut job recluses. Bechet couldn't blame Braxton for not wanting to claim any part of that Cross legacy. Bechet had no intention of it either.

Another reason pulling off this deal with Kevin and the Corinthian was a big deal for him. It was his way of proving he wasn't any less capable or worthy of the Cross lineage, just because he didn't want to fuck with the spirits of Sowell Gate Mountains. He pushed the thought aside and focused on the work in front of him. The sooner he got this done, the sooner he would get to see Isis again.

Isis dragged herself into her apartment, letting her bag fall to the floor with a thud. She was exhausted from door-knocking almost all day. She had only meant to be out for a few hours, not the entire day, but something about mixing and mingling with the people always made her lose track of time.

The reward for her hard work would be the continued trust of her constituents. Half of the people whose door she knocked on had talked her ear off about the mayor's mistress scandal. Had been pleased that they 'never had to worry' about her being like those entitled male politicians. On the one hand, she enjoyed knowing that they believed in her integrity. On the other, it only cemented the sad state of her dating life. What would her constituents think if the details behind her disastrous relationship with Richard ever trickled beyond the country club circle?

Dating another politician was out of the question, even before the scandal. Now with this whole mayoral affair, Isis would have to be much more careful with who and how she was seen going forward. Not only to keep her marriage-minded grandmother off her back, but to keep her almost spotless reputation intact. The last thing she needed was to be seen as another woman sleeping her way through the political arena.

It sucked, but that was the reality of her job. A harsh reality only made harsher by the mayor's scandal and women like the married councilwoman who had attempted to do just that. Isis tried not to let it get to her, not to let it demoralize her or make her rethink her goals in life. She'd known all of this before deciding to go into politics. This was her dream. She would do anything to keep it alive.

Her misstep with Richard aside, Isis would have to work even harder to remain above reproach. Her privacy was tantamount.

She slipped off her sneakers and deposited them right in the trash. The soles were completely worn down, and the left shoe even had a hole in the bottom at this point. She got herself a glass of water before stripping on her way to her bedroom. A nice long shower was exactly what she needed, and then she would figure out dinner.

The thought of dinner sent a jolt of panic through her body.

"Fuck, Bechet," she cursed, turning her wrist up to check her watch.

It was 6:45PM, way too late to cancel as he was probably already on his way. She rushed through a quick shower and had just enough time to slip into a cute pink lounge set before there was a knock on her door. She took a deep breath and put on a smile she hoped didn't look as tired as she felt before opening the door.

Bechet stood there in a pair of tan slacks and a light blue t-shirt. He looked relaxed and bright-eyed as he held up the bag in his hand.

"I hope you like Chinese," he said.

Isis nodded. "I love it," she said and gestured for him to come in.

He went right to her kitchen and set the food on her counter. She opened the cabinet and pulled out plates.

"You look comfortable," Bechet said.

Isis froze mid-reach and looked over her shoulder. Ready to tear into him for his rude comment, only to stop when she saw Bechet was staring at her ass. He licked his lips, and his Adam's apple bobbed as he swallowed. She shook her head before grabbing what she needed and bringing it to the counter.

"You are terrible with compliments," she laughed.

Bechet had the nerve to blush. "I am amazing at compliments. It's you that gets me so tongue-tied," Bechet said.

"Tongue-tied? Really," she breathed.

Bechet nodded, his eyes darkening with desire. Her nipples hardened under his gaze. They stared at each other for a moment. The air crackled with sexual tension. Her lips parted, and her breathing shallowed. Bechet pulled her into his arms, moving in slow motion. His face came closer and closer to hers.

Isis closed her eyes as their lips touched. Bechet's tongue teased the seam of her lips. She moaned as her body melted into his. While Isis appreciated him trying to take things slow, her own desire pushed her to go further and move faster. She didn't hesitate to slide her hand between them and cup him through his slacks. He growled, and she pushed him toward the couch. They sank as one into the pillowy cushions.

Bechet grew large and thick as Isis continued to fondle him. He cupped the back of her head, deepening the kiss, their tongues meeting a sensual duel. Bechet continued his oral onslaught while reaching down to fondle her breast, slipping it free from her skimpy top. His rough hands rasped so deliciously against her sensitive nipple. Isis cried out when he gave it a light pinch before trailing his hand down her body to the v between her legs. She moaned and wiggled against his touch as he slipped his hand into her panties and circled her clit. Her hips rocked into his touch.

Isis continued to stroke him over his pants. As much as she would love to feel how slick and warm his cock would be, she knew that once she did, there would be no going back. She wasn't entirely against the idea of them having sex. It had been much longer than Isis cared to admit since she'd had anything but her own fingers or something that run on batteries between her legs.

"Fuck, Isis. Slow down, baby," Bechet gasped.

"I'll slow down when you do," she sighed.

Isis continued her slow stroking of his dick, egging Bechet on as he used his fingers in just the right places on her inner walls to have her clinging to him and crying out. Isis was experienced, but none of her past lovers compared. Bechet played her body like it was his favorite guitar, knowing exactly where and just how to pluck or strum or caress to make the perfect notes of a perfect song.

"Hell no, I want to see if your O face is as perfect as I imagine," Bechet said.

Isis came so hard on his fingers alone that she was afraid if he was only half as good with what was clearly his very large cock, she would die in his arms a happy woman. That thought was enough to keep Isis in check. She had agreed to a no-strings fling, and feelings were the ultimate in strings. She had to make sure she could keep her emotions in check before they got to the fucking part of their arrangement. They needed to clarify a few more details about that anyway. She couldn't be caught off guard again like she had been with Richard; the current political climate would not allow for her to make such a major misstep a second time.

Despite her logical mind making valid points as to why she should slow this down, why she should stop this before things went too far, Isis wanted him to go further. She was putty in his hands, but instead, Bechet seemed to be much more in control of himself. He stopped as soon as the last shudders of climax left her. He removed his fingers from inside her, and she watched as he licked them clean.

"Fuck, you're beautiful and delicious," he groaned.

Isis smirked, a witty comeback on her tongue, but then the weight of Bechet's body was gone from hers. She blinked a few times, and he was back in the kitchen, rummaging through the takeout bags and setting out the food.

"Where are you going?" she sputtered.

Her body was still all warm and tingly from her orgasm. She craved more of his touch. More of the intimacy that had been so thick between them just seconds ago.

"We should eat before it gets cold," he said.

Isis bit her lip. If anything was cold, it was him. How could he be so hot one minute and then shut it off like nothing happened? She sat up and adjusted her clothing, so all her goodies were covered once more. She took that time to pull herself together. Of course, Bechet was able to switch gears so fast. This was nothing more than a business arrangement.

She meant nothing to him, would never mean anything to him, and the sooner she understood that, the better.

❖❖ · ·◆· · ❖❖

Bechet kept his eyes off Isis as he served up the takeout he'd brought. He knew if he looked at her now, he would have no choice but to take her right there on her couch. His heart was still racing, his dick pressing hard against his inseam. If it was only lust he felt, he might not care, but there was something else. Something a lot more concerning.

"Do you want to eat at the table or on the couch?"

Bechet forced his gaze up to meet hers. Isis had moved from the couch and was now standing beside him. The heat radiated from her body like a siren's call. His fingers itched to touch her again, to feel her soft skin, to bury his face at the crook of her neck, or, better yet, in the sweet musky heat between her legs.

"Uh, the table is fine," he said and quickly brought the plates over to the small wooden table in the corner.

The table was safe, and the couch was most definitely not. Bechet needed to handle whatever this new thing he was feeling was before he could trust himself to further explore their physical attraction. He'd made that mistake with Rachel. Letting his libido drive him and not seeing the way Rachel had begun to insinuate herself into his life. Making friends with his mother behind his back, setting up a position for him with her father's company because she didn't see the whole 'furniture thing', as she called it, panning out.

"Alright, what would you like to drink? I have water, tea, or wine," Isis offered.

Bechet snorted with laughter, glad for the interruption into his trip to the land of unwanted relationships past. At least he knew that Isis wouldn't do those things to him. He'd asked Dom about her when he realized she was *the* Isis Hale. The rising star of local politics and former debutante. Dom's shop was gossip central, and when her best friend Jay wasn't around, the talk about her was more about her power moves and cool demeanor, than any sugar baby tendencies.

"Water is fine," he said.

"I had a long day and didn't have time to really prepare for guests," Isis said, taking the chair across from him.

The distance was too close and yet too far. Bechet took a good look at her and noticed for the first time the exhaustion on her face. The sudden urge to pull her into his lap and massage the weariness from her body overcame him like a tsunami. He rubbed his chest before Isis took his hand in hers. She said grace over the food and began to eat.

"I apologize if my last-minute request is a burden," Bechet managed.

Isis stopped eating to shake her head. "No, it's fine. If I didn't want to meet with you, I wouldn't have said yes," Isis said.

"Still, I don't want to overstay my welcome. We'll eat and chat, but then I'll get out of your hair. We can reconnect again over the weekend when you have more time," Bechet said.

Isis' eyes went from warm and sleepy to hard and cold.

"If that's what you want," she said.

Bechet had no idea why he couldn't seem to get things right with Isis. He was always saying the wrong things, or even when he said something he didn't think was wrong, she'd shut down, like right now. If he were in any way capable of logic where Isis was concerned, he would get up and leave now. Cut his losses and find another willing and more easily read partner. Yet, there was nothing logical or straightforward about whatever was happening between him and Isis. No matter what they said about their wants or what they had agreed, things were obviously not simple and stringless as promised.

Hoping to brighten her mood, Bechet turned the topic of conversation to the latest political headlines. To be honest, Bechet rarely paid attention to politics, but he was an avid reader of the paper, and the current mayoral scandal had been plastered right up front.

"How is your office handling the mayor's scandal. Does it have any effect at your level of politics?"

Isis's eyes flashed with a combination of anger and frustration.

"Any political scandal affects all levels. Canvasing and face time with the public is my happy place usually, and those assholes made that less joyful today," she said.

"How so?"

"Well, it's not fun to try talking to people about the real issues affecting the community, when all they want to talk about is who the mayor is fucking and why. It's frustrating."

"I could see how that could be less than ideal. Why did you spend all day out if it was that bad?"

Isis sighed.

"Because I need to keep my face out of the mud. I needed them to see that despite the scandal, someone, namely me, was focused on the real issues. That my integrity was above reproach."

"What the mayor did was shitty, but that doesn't mean he wasn't doing his job. I honestly think it's ridiculous how obsessed people are with politicians' love lives," Bechet admitted.

"It's the scourge of our society. Sex sells, and if you are a person of any notoriety or import, your sex life is seen as fair game. You know this; otherwise, you wouldn't be so into these discreet social relationships," Isis said.

Bechet nodded.

"Very true. Cheers to discreet agreements and avoiding the bullshit," Bechet said raising his glass.

Isis chuckled and raised her glass as well. "To avoiding the bullshit," she said.

Bechet even stayed a little longer than he had originally planned to chat with her. He learned that she had hated being a debutante. That while she hoped to marry one day, her focus was on her career. A sentiment she and Bechet shared. He shared with her a bit more about his goals for Cross logging and why he was in Mulberry. He may have imagined it, but she'd seemed a little sad that he was only a Mulberry resident for a third of the year. Staying for maybe a month each quarter, just long enough for him to do some business before heading home to Edgewood.

It wasn't until Isis fell asleep on his shoulder that Bechet reluctantly took his leave. He stood for a moment, cradling her in his arms, before he took her into her bedroom and tucked her into bed. Something he'd never done with any woman before. Especially not one he hadn't just had sex with. He placed a soft kiss on her cheek before leaving her to sleep.

Bechet knew then that this was not going to be just a simple arrangement between the two of them. He was notoriously unattached when it came to women, but Isis had found a way under his skin quickly. He would have to keep his distance until Saturday; otherwise, there would be no salvaging the terms they had both agreed to.

CHAPTER THREE

That Saturday, Isis spent way more time than she should have to pick out just the right outfit for the evening. Normally these things would have been done well in advance, but Isis hadn't exactly been on her A-game this week. She'd been too busy either daydreaming about Bechet's fine ass or berating herself for being so caught up in a man she barely knew. It didn't help that Bechet had continued to text her throughout the week, asking about her day, sending her silly jokes or articles about things she might be interested in. As much as he had said he wanted a no-strings affair, this last week had shown that neither Isis or he had any idea what that actually meant. One thing was for sure, Isis would need to be careful with Bechet. She needed to keep her guard up; otherwise, this whole situation was just one big recipe for disaster.

Isis had just finished putting the last touches on her hair and makeup when the doorbell rang. She grabbed her purse and shoes before heading to the door. Isis thought she'd know what to expect when she opened it. He'd texted her the color and style of his suit in advance to make sure it wouldn't clash with her outfit choice. Another first for Isis, usually she was the one who fussed over those sorts of details. It also wasn't her first time seeing Bechet in a suit. He'd been wearing one when they first met. One of the reasons she'd gone along with having him as her date, she already knew he could dress to impress. Shockingly, she was completely unprepared for the insanely handsome man standing on her doorstep.

"Evening. You look fantastic," he said.

Isis fought the urge to melt at his feet as arousal crept through her body. He had on a standard tux with a white shirt and black tie. Yet, it looked anything but standard on him. Bechet stood at her door with the swoon-worthy smirk she could only attribute to the likes of Denzel, Morris, and Idris before then. She noted the change in his cologne. This time, it held a bit more musk that, while subtle, made her want to invite him inside instead of exiting her apartment like she forced her legs to do.

"Thank you, you too," she said, hoping he wouldn't notice how flustered she was by his looks.

Bechet took her arm before leading her out to his car. It was a Bentley coupe, and certainly not what she had expected him to show up in, and part of her wondered if it was a rental for the evening. They were going to a pretty high-profile charity ball that coincidentally happened to be in the grand ballroom of a hotel, just two blocks from where they met. There would be professional athletes, politicians, and even a few movie stars in attendance.

Isis' mother had shunned her debutante upbringing, but her grandmother had insisted Isis follow in her footsteps. Granted, she had never wanted or felt the need to be just a pretty fixture on anyone's arm. Her focus had already moved beyond that and into the political arena, which was another reason to not show up to this event alone. It sucked, but a single woman her age just wasn't taken seriously unless she had her own powerful arm candy as a backup.

"Is this event for show or for work?" Bechet asked.

Isis sighed. Bechet already knew the answer. They had discussed it over text earlier in the week. He had probably noticed her nerves and was trying to break the tension. Part of her loved that he was clearly trying to calm her before the event. The other part was pissed that she was still emoting too much.

"Both; being charitable is always a good look as a politician, but it's also a place to mingle with potential donors and keeps my grandmother off my back about most of the more mundane society events around town."

Bechet chuckled, "I feel you on that, only it's my mother who wishes I was more into the societal life. If she knew I was going to such a public charity event, I think she would literally jump for joy. Anyway, I'm happy to be your arm candy tonight, even if I would normally avoid this type of thing like the plague."

"What? You not charitable, Mr. Cross?"

"I make plenty of donations. I just don't care for the whole keeping up with the Joneses vibe."

Isis laughed. "I can agree with that much. Anyway, thanks again for coming. I could have come alone, but that puts so much extra work into the evening. Especially with my ex being on the guest list."

Bechet just nodded and didn't ask Isis to clarify her statement. Isis wasn't sure if that meant he understood what she meant or that he just didn't care. They had talked a little about the pressure of being a single female politician over dinner on Monday, but Isis hadn't explicitly stated her concerns about being seen as just another woman sleeping her way to the top. Nor had she mentioned anything about Richard being another reason she hadn't wanted to come alone. His silence only fueled her doubt.

"Who says you won't be putting some extra work in this evening," Bechet said with a wink.

"Was that supposed to be a sex joke?"

"I don't joke about sex, but don't worry. I'll be your shield against the gossips and Richard. If tonight goes as planned, we'll both be working hard all night long," he replied.

His crudeness as well as the fact he somehow knew about Richard shocked her. Once again, there was this disconnect between them. Sometimes she felt like he knew exactly what she was dealing with. He obviously was connected enough to be a patron at Westmoore's Barbershop and be a client of Dominic Westmoore himself. Which now that she thought about it was probably where he'd heard about Richard. Then again, she had never heard of any Cross's in Mulberry's Society Life.

At the same time that he talked about family estates, he also didn't have the same air about him as the wealthy men she usually came across. Maybe his family's money was new. It would explain his mother's excitement about him getting into societal life. Mulberry wasn't as pretentious as other areas, but it didn't mean there weren't barriers to entry. Isis's own family, while established and well off, still wasn't held with the same regard as the Westmoore's.

"You're frowning," Bechet said.

Isis blinked a few times and smiled.

"Sorry, just running scenarios for the evening. I wish I could say that I don't have people besides my ex that I'd rather not deal with tonight, but it's always a possibility."

It wasn't entirely a lie. There were people she wasn't looking forward to seeing. Kevin, for one. That would really ruin her evening. Yet her frowning had more to do with his lewd suggestions than any of that. Maybe he wasn't so far removed from Kevin as she thought.

Maybe that was why she had such a hard time reconciling her attraction to Bechet. For all, she knew he could be lying to her about who he was and what he did for a living. He was still a stranger. An extremely sexy stranger that seemed to know just how to get through her defenses.

Bechet smiled back at her. "Not a problem. If the scenario pops up, just give my arm a squeeze, and I'll whisk you off to the dance floor."

Isis laughed and shoved down the creeping suspicion in her gut. She was over-critical, exactly like Jay said. She was attracted to Bechet, and that scared her, so she was finding every little thing to pick at and dissect. She needed to stop. Whatever happened with her and Bechet, she decided right then and there that it wouldn't be because she had picked the man to death in her mind before anything really got started between them.

"I'll keep that in mind."

Having Bechet as her date was looking like it just might be better for her than she anticipated. He would be an unknown, and having him on her arm would be seen as a power play. They pulled up to the event, and Bechet helped Isis out of the car after handing his key over to the valet. There were more paparazzi at the event than Isis expected, and her appearance on the small red carpet usually didn't garner much attention. Bechet stepped aside, allowing for her to be photographed alone before stepping in again so they could take one together. Something none of her previous dates ever did, not even Jay.

Again, Bechet was showing her so many desirable traits that she was afraid that she had bitten off more than she could chew in terms of their arrangement. They moved quickly inside after the obligatory photo op.

Isis was pleasantly surprised with how Bechet handled himself. He stayed by her side but didn't try to butt into her conversations or talk over her. He didn't even make a fool of himself or her when it came to the sportsmen in the building. She really shouldn't be surprised, she supposed. If he was a client at Westmoore's, he was used to rubbing elbows with different professionals and power brokers. Isis had also been very clear about her motives in inviting him to this event. It was nice to spend time with a man who could take guidance without his ego getting in the way.

They moved into the grand ballroom where the event was being held. It was quieter here, away from the fussiness of the press area and entryway. Isis spotted her first target of the night. Connor Abernathy was a major political donor who had recently pulled his support of the mayor due to the scandal. She'd met him once or twice before, but had never gotten the chance to really show her stuff as a potential politician for him to back. She gently tugged at Bechet's arm to move toward the group of people Abernathy was chatting with, but stopped as she noticed that her entrance into the room hadn't gone unnoticed as it usually would have.

What she didn't expect was the pure shock and awe of some people who had barely given her the time of day before. They seemed to flock in their direction, impeding their progress toward Abernathy. Only instead of talking to her, they were more interested in Bechet. By the time the crowd parted, the lights were being dimmed for the presentation portion of the night, which meant there was nothing they could do but find their assigned table. Isis sat stewing the tidbit of information she'd gleaned from the unexpected interactions.

It was pretty clear that the people she had hoped to woo on her own terms, now saw her as purely Bechet's arm candy for the evening. Not a single person seemed interested in discussing anything with her beyond her choice in shoes or dress. Isis could barely pay attention to the program being put on and picked at the 20-thousand-dollar plate of rubbery catered chicken. The more she thought about it, the more pissed she became. As soon as it wasn't overtly rude to do so, Isis excused herself to the bathroom.

She made a show of fixing her makeup, while really she was using every tool in her arsenal to calm the fuck down. She spiraled in her own self-doubt. She hadn't felt this way in years, not since she'd left the debutante circle. There was just something about the way the people in her family's world treated women. As commodities, pretty fixtures adorn a man's arm and boost his ego. It was all too much for Isis. Had always been.

"Are you okay?"

Isis looked up to see Rachel Headley standing next to her. The statuesque blonde had been the top debutante of Isis's time. They had never been friends, and Isis found the woman's sudden interest in Isis suspicious.

"Yes, just avoiding all those carbs, you know." Isis giggled, falling back into the role she'd cast aside once she left the debutante circle.

Rachel smiled back. "Oh, it's good you are finally taking charge of your weight issues. I mean, you've slimmed down a lot from back in the day. It's obviously been helpful in your marriage prospects," she replied.

Isis wanted to smack the smug smile off the woman's face, but instead, she tucked her makeup back into her clutch. "It was nice seeing you, Rachel. I should be getting back to my date."

"Oh, and do give Chet my regards. It's been ages since we've chatted," Rachel called after her.

Isis just kept moving toward the door, choosing not to read too much into the fact that Rachel was still a bitch after all these years and that she was apparently well acquainted with Bechet. The thought bothered her way too much for it to be wise for Isis to dwell on. She was already stretching herself thin in the social butterfly department. Maybe coming to this event with Bechet had been a mistake.

The lights in the ballroom had been brought back up, and the plates had been cleared, yet most of the people in attendance were still chatting at their tables instead of the dance floor. Isis started to return to the table but saw that

Bechet had no trouble at all chatting it up with the others. She suddenly wasn't in the mood to sit any longer. Instead, she moved toward the bank of windows to stare out at the night skyline. Bechet joined her. Sliding his arm around her waist, he moved them in a swaying motion to the soft music that was playing.

It would have been romantic, if not for the million and one questions Isis now had about the man she was starting to get attached to. Still, she couldn't help being caught up in the moment. The lovely view of the city lights below them, the feel of him pressed against her back. She let her head relax against his chest, and he spun her around. Pulling her away from the window and to the dance floor. They danced until all the tension had melted from her body. She looked up at Bechet, getting lost in his heated gaze. His face inched closer to hers, his beard tickling her cheeks and upper lip before his mouth pressed to hers. A soft, innocent peck, but it sent hot molten lava straight to her core. Bechet pulled away and whispered in her ear.

"Tell me what's bothering you."

All the frustration Bechet had managed to soothe earlier came back with a vengeance.

"I didn't realize you were so connected," Isis said.

"Well, the Westmoores are a fixture in this town. I told you I usually avoid these events. My cousin Dom is much more suited to handle all the schmoozing," he said.

All the missing pieces fell into place then. Isis couldn't help but pull away from him in shock.

"You're a Westmoore?" she sputtered.

He chuckled and pulled her back into his embrace. Making the whole scenario seem like an orchestrated dance move instead of Isis freaking out.

"I'm a little offended that you are so shocked," he said.

Isis quickly regained her composure. "Sorry. I just didn't make the connection," she said.

Bechet smiled and spun her out before bringing her back against his body.

"That's more than fine. I mean, the Cross name isn't as well known, and I try not to use my Westmoore connections unless absolutely necessary," he answered.

"No, it really isn't fine," Isis said, and his smile faltered.

Isis was panicking. She could feel the unwanted emotion trickling into her veins and initiating her flight response. She did her best to tamp it down, but it was still there, pressing forcefully at her control measures.

"How is it not?" Bechet asked, picking up on her dismay.

"If I had known, I never would have come with you," Isis immediately cringed, seeing his smile fade completely.

Where were her impeccable social skills when she needed them? Isis could admit she tended to be blunt but never this rude. There was just something about Bechet that seemed to get under her skin. Something that reached beyond her carefully crafted walls and weathered them to dust. Then to make matters worse, her gut reaction was to put her whole ass foot in her mouth. She didn't mean to be so aggressive and cold.

"You should be grateful I put myself out here like this," he said in an even tone.

Isis knew she should say something. Try to explain, but for once in her life, the words just wouldn't come. She pulled away from him again and started to walk away. He didn't try to pull her back, and when she turned to see if he followed, Mitsy Abernathy was now in his arms. It was an added insult to injury. She finally had her chance to get Mr. Abernathy alone, and it was all because his beautiful young daughter was now happily flirting in the arms of Isis' date.

She turned back toward the exit only to run smack into her ex Richard, and on his arm was a smiling Rachel Headley.

"Isis! I'm surprised to see you here," Richard said.

Isis didn't miss the smug look of satisfaction on his face as his gaze traveled from Bechet and Mitsy back to her. Isis had assumed he would be at the event, but when he hadn't appeared before dinner was served, she assumed he was going to be a no-show. It also explained why she had only run into Rachel in the bathroom and not before. It was tacky to show up so late to a charity event like this, and Isis could only assume he'd shown up after hearing that she had arrived with Bechet.

"Oh, Richard, you know I would never miss a charity event," she replied, pasting on her best fake smile.

"Richard, darling, are you going to introduce us?" Rachel asked, pawing at his arm like a cat.

"Are introductions really necessary, Rachel?" Isis was too angry at this point to be more polite.

"In this case, yes. Isis, Rachel is my fiancé," Richard said.

Rachel extended her hand, flashing the gaudy cluster of diamonds of the ring Isis had found in Richard's drawer just before they'd ended things. Isis felt like she'd just been slapped in the face. Not because she cared that Richard and Rachel were together and obviously had been even before Richard had ended things with Isis. She just really wasn't prepared for this particular turn of events.

She needed to leave. She needed to exit the building before this became more of a scene than it already was, yet her feet wouldn't move. People around them who had done a very poor job of not eavesdropping on their conversation began to come over and congratulate the new couple.

Isis was a firm believer in acknowledging everyone with respect, even if the other woman wasn't someone Isis actually respected. So she properly oohed and ahhed over the ring with the other women and offered a not so heartfelt congratulations. Rachel's smug smile faltered a little as her eyes were drawn to something behind Isis. Isis could almost see the calculated desire in the woman's eyes before she smelled

Bechet's intoxicating cologne and felt his arm slide around her waist.

"Isis, I hate to interrupt your mingling, but we have to be on our way," Bechet said tersely before shooting a less than friendly grin at Richard and Rachel and dragging Isis toward the door.

"What the hell was that?" Isis said once in his car, and he just glared at her.

"I could ask you the same thing," Bechet snapped.

"I have no idea what you are even talking about, and I don't appreciate your tone," Isis snapped back.

"My tone? You take issue with my tone after having a whole ass attitude all night. An attitude that was nowhere to be found when you were fawning all over your ex?"

"I was not fawning, and maybe if you hadn't fucking lied to me about who you were, tonight would have gone much smoother," Isis said.

"I have no idea what your problem is. I took a big risk accompanying you tonight, and I get nothing but attitude and disrespect in return," Bechet grumbled.

Isis was pissed off, and she knew that now probably wasn't the best time to try and explain just how fucked up this whole situation was. Yet, she couldn't help herself. Any other man and she would have asked him to pull over so she could find her own ride home, yet she felt she owed Bechet some sort of explanation. Even if he was a total asshole. Now would probably be her chance to explain herself. Isis knew when she was wrong, and she was woman enough to admit it. Whatever happened after that was out of her control.

"I'm not trying to be rude, and I know you don't come to these things, and that is exactly the problem. Everyone will think I am only where I am because I am sleeping with you," she said, and he scoffed.

"Seriously? That's your big issue? That people will think we are fucking," he said, shaking his head.

"We talked about this when we discussed the mayor's scandal. You're a man. It's perfectly okay to have everyone all in your sex life, but for me, it's basically the kiss of death. No one will take me seriously now that I've been seen in a romantic capacity with you."

He turned the radio on and didn't say a word to Isis the entire drive back to her building. He didn't even walk her to her door. Instead, he just pulled up to the front of the building and nodded for her to get out.

"I would say it was a lovely evening, but..."

He didn't have to finish the sentence. Whatever thing had been budding between them had been thoroughly squashed. Isis was done. She couldn't believe she was foolish enough to think that anyone involved with Kevin could be anything but trouble. Her conclusion was cemented by the fact that Bechet didn't even wait for Isis to go inside before he pulled off.

Bechet was pissed as he raced down the street and away from Isis's building. It wasn't like he lived far, but he also wasn't heading home. Bechet was too angry to be alone. He hit the autodial button for his cousin Dom, a little surprised that he answered at this time of night.

"Hey, man! Date end early?" Dom chuckled.

Bechet's grip on the steering wheel tightened, turning his knuckles white. "Yeah, you could say that. What are you up to?"

"Nothing, just hanging out at the rooftop lounge," Dom said.

"Great, I'll see you there."

Bechet hung up before his cousin could ask any more questions. He knew he was only delaying the inevitable, but he'd rather converse over a much-needed drink.

You have no right to be angry.

Bechet's conscience tugged at him. It didn't matter if Isis had every reason to be upset about tonight. Hell, he even knew that her anger wasn't about Bechet at all but about the shitty standards society held women like her to. The real reason he was so pissed? Her rejection. No matter how things started between them, Bechet was only just now realizing he wanted more than the agreement he'd made with Isis. He actually wanted a relationship with her, and she, for somewhat valid reasons, didn't want shit to do with him.

To top it all off, he'd had to see Rachel again. He was glad she finally got what she wanted, but hated that it was with the man who had hurt Isis. There had been a few rumors about her relationship to the man that he'd heard at Westmoore's but he hadn't paid it much attention at the time. Isis had been merely a stranger, a woman he had wanted to bed and not much else. So he'd only noted the man's name.

He hated that he hadn't paid more attention. Maybe he could have reacted better, done something to block her from the man's obvious attempt at making Isis seem small and inconsequential.

Bechet's grip on the wheel tightened at the image of the man smiling smugly at Isis as he introduced Rachel as his fiancé. To Isis' credit, she had managed to keep her cool. She did a good job of acting happy and congratulating the couple at the ball but he'd seen the flash of anger and pain before her mask slid into place. That alone told Bechet all he needed to know about Isis' commitment to keeping appearances. His mother would love her if they ever got the chance to meet.

Meeting my mother? Bechet, you've seriously lost it.

Bechet sped around the corner and pulled to a screeching halt in front of the valet at K Hotel, not caring a bit about the stares as he tossed the man his keys and jogged over to the elevators that would take him to the lounge. It wasn't until the elevator closed on him and the crush of bodies headed up for a good time, that Bechet realized Isis may have had a point. His actions just now were the opposite of anything she would be okay with. He should just let her go.

The rooftop lounge at K Hotel was crowded as usual, but Dom was easily spotted in the VIP area. Not because he was doing anything more than sipping his scotch, but because Kevin was there with him. Kevin was the last person he wanted to hang out with right now, but it was already too late for him to turn around and pretend he hadn't come.

Kevin spotted him and waved him over, so Bechet reluctantly joined him and the sea of groupies playing pick me at his side. At least, Kevin didn't seem interested in chatting it up, turning his attention to his female fans and leaving Bechet and Dom to themselves.

"So, your date with Isis," Dom said with a smirk.

Bechet scowled.

"I have no idea what the hell I'm going to do with that woman. She's sweet and enjoyable one moment, and the next..." Bechet groaned.

Kevin laughed and handed Bechet a glass of vodka over ice.

"Frigid, hard as ice. Isis comes by the nickname, honestly. I'll give you that," Kevin supplied.

Bechet set the drink down carefully as not to give away the sudden spike in anger he felt at Kevin's comments. Isis could be icy at times, but to be fair, with Bechet, it hadn't all been without reason, and knowing Kevin, Isis wouldn't suffer a fool like him at all. The man's observations shouldn't bother Bechet anyway. Isis had nothing to do with him, would have nothing to do with him, especially after tonight.

"Don't listen to him. Look, Isis is a hard one, and maybe too hard for what you are looking for. Don't let it get to you," Dom offered.

Bechet wanted to tell his cousin that he didn't know what he was talking about. That Isis was exactly what he wanted. He also wanted to punch Kevin just on principle for talking about his woman. Except Isis wasn't truly his, and that was precisely the damn problem.

"You're right. I am a little over-invested for my liking. It's just I'm used to being insulted because of the Cross name. Never for being a Westmoore," Bechet admitted.

Dom raised an eyebrow at that.

"Wait, you're saying she cut you off because you're my cousin?"

"Not exactly, and it's complicated. She's worried about her image. Being seen as using me to further her career ambitions," Bechet said.

Dom shook his head. "What the fuck does that even mean? I know she's into politics but not at a level where the Westmoore's would even bother endorsing. On top of that, if she wants to get serious, she will need our family's support."

Bechet sat back with a shrug. "I don't even pretend to understand the inner workings of politicians and their reputations. Anyway, not only did she take issue with me not being explicit about being a Westmoore, her ex showed up flaunting his new fiancé."

Dom shook his head. "Richard? I doubt Isis really gave a shit about that. I mean, I don't really know her like that, but she doesn't strike me as the type to get all green-eyed over a man she was done with."

"You sure she was done with him?"

"Oh yeah, he was a prick and cheated on her. She holds a grudge like nobody's business but is definitely more the cold shoulder type. I'm betting if she seemed angry, it's because he's engaged to Rachel Headley. Isis hates her almost as much as she hates me," Kevin butted in.

Dom scowled at Kevin before raising an eyebrow at Bechet. "Rachel was there? You sure Isis didn't pick up on anything between you two?"

Now it was Bechet's turn to scowl. "You know damn well I feel nothing for that conniving bitch. Hell, if anything, I'm happy some poor sap finally gave her what she wanted."

"Mmhmm, I'm sure that's the reason," Kevin muttered another unwanted opinion.

"Anyway, give Isis the rest of the weekend so both of you can chill. Give you both some time to think real hard about it. You want to continue whatever the hell it is you two have going," Dom said.

"Fuck that man, I say, cut and run. Hell, you already know I got your back if you need some discrete companionship. No need to deal with Isis' crazy ass," Kevin said.

Bechet shook his head. "I'm done talking. I can deal with the drama later," Bechet said and downed his drink.

Dom nodded. "Probably for the best. You still coming to the pick-up game tomorrow before Alicia's party?"

"Yeah, I'll be there," Bechet said before ordering another drink.

CHAPTER FOUR

There was someone banging on her door. Isis groaned and looked at her clock. It was eight in the morning. Early for most people, especially on a Sunday, but not for her. Isis usually woke up around six. The fact she was still in bed all crusty-eyed told her she'd been more affected by last night than she thought. The banging sounded again, and she groaned.

Who the fuck is at my door at this hour?

The answer was pretty much anybody. For the most part, her neighbors were quiet and kept to themselves, until they didn't. There was one other young woman in her building who had a constant stream of boyfriends who liked to get drunk and have long-winded chats about why she'd broken their hearts. Occasionally they were so drunk, they ended up at Isis's door instead of hers. Isis grabbed her phone to call the cops, not wanting to deal with the drama, only to see she'd missed a few messages from Jay.

He was the asshole banging on her door because she'd sent him a drunken text last night that she shouldn't have. She got up and opened the door for him before her neighbors called the cops about the noise. The last thing she needed on top of last night's disaster was a police report about yet another angry Black man tied to her.

"What did he do?" he asked.

"Sorry about the text. It's nothing. I'm fine," Isis said.

Jay studied her for a moment before shaking his head. "You are not fine. That text was bullshit. How dare you accuse me of throwing you under the bus. I didn't make you go with Bechet. You chose that asshole," Jay said.

Isis sighed. "I already apologized for the text. Yes, I was the one who chose Bechet, but how could you not warn me he was a Westmoore!" she said, and Jay rolled his eyes.

"How clueless can you be, Isis? Everyone knows he is Dom's cousin. Hell, how bad was last night? Do I need to worry about going to work tomorrow?" he asked.

"Are you afraid you're going to get fired or blackballed because of me?" Isis asked, and Jay gave her an incredulous look.

"No, Dom and the shop have nothing to do with this. I mean, am I going to be fighting people tomorrow because you fell right into bed with the man who taught Kevin all his slimy ways?" he said.

That bit of information made Isis clutch her stomach. She'd known a little about his relationship with Kevin, but he'd made it seem all business. Isis felt even more played now that she knew the truth and even angrier because Jay was just now telling her. If she'd known, she could have avoided this whole situation.

"Seriously? You had days to tell me this information before last night. That he was a Westmoore, and that he was closer to Kevin than he told me," she said.

"Look, I knew you two had a date, but I honestly thought you would have figured it out on your own," he said, and she sighed.

"You know how marriage-minded my grandmother is. You should have told me who he was before letting me accept him as a stand-in."

Jay just shook his head. "Geez, Isis. Take some responsibility for this. One minute you're up my ass about staying out of your dating life, and now you've got me in a bind because I was trying to do the adult thing and give you space. This is messed up on so many levels. I feel like I'm on an episode of Love and Mulberry Heights. If you are going to keep seeing him be careful and try not to get our grandmothers all worked up about it."

"Thanks for the concern, Jay, but I doubt I will be seeing him again after last night. You're right. I was able to figure it out on my own. Bechet Cross is not anyone I should be associating with."

Isis hated how dejected she sounded by the idea, but it was too late to change that now. Jay's eyes softened with concern.

"Look, Isis. I love you like a sister and never want to see you get hurt. Did he try anything with you? Do I need to go rearrange his face? I can run him out of town if you want, Westmoore or not."

She couldn't help but smile at that. Jay was her best friend for a reason. Even when he was annoyingly male. "No, looking back on the evening he was perfect. Better than anyone else I could have brought with me aside from the whole being a bald-faced liar. Ugh, this is so frustrating. I will take responsibility for not doing my due diligence with Bechet before Saturday, and I am sorry you got dragged into this mess."

Jay smirked. "If you are really sorry, you will bake me some of your famous cupcakes."

Of course, Jay would do anything to get her to bake, and it was one of her few domestic hobbies.

"Why should I?" Isis asked, and Jay glared at her.

"Because you interrupted my plans with Charlotte, and she said if I don't get at least one cupcake from you, she will never forgive me," he said.

"You're lucky I'm in a baking mood," she muttered before a big grin spread across her face. "Should I leave room for a ring on one of these cupcakes for you? The way you've been acting lately, I'd think you were about to ask Charlotte to marry you."

Jay shrugged and looked away. His cheeks glowed as he tried to fight a nervous smile. "Don't worry about all that. Just cupcakes, please. You can stop by Monday around closing."

Isis shook her head. "To be clear, these cupcakes are an apology to Charlotte for messing up her plans. I will drop them at her office to ensure she gets them fresh."

"Fine, fine. Apology accepted. Now I've got to get back to my woman before she really throws a fit," Jay gave her a quick hug before leaving.

Isis was exhausted, but the thought of baking enough sugar bombs to cover her massive kitchen island was enough to get her moving. Nothing cleared her mind and soothed her spirit more than making delicious confections to share with her loved ones. It was the perfect task to get her mind off the disaster of last night and the major bullet named Bechet Cross she had just dodged.

But the universe had other plans. As soon as Isis pulled out the butter and eggs to bring to room temperature, her phone began to ring. Since Jay had shown up at her house already, she knew the only person who'd dare disturb her this early on the weekend was her grandmother.

"Good morning," Isis did her best to sound cheerful.

"We have brunch this morning at the Regency. 10:30, don't be late," Willa Tremaine said.

"10:30? That's a little earlier than—" Isis began, but Willa cut her off.

"Don't sass me, young lady. I'll see you soon," Willa said and hung up.

With a groan, Isis put the butter and eggs back in the fridge. Baking and her happiness would have to wait a few more hours. She shouldn't have been so surprised when her grandmother called demanding to see her. They usually caught up over Sunday brunch, but Isis had been bailing recently, to avoid being set up by her grandmother. She knew this day would come sooner rather than later, and after last night's fiasco, it wasn't a far stretch that Willa Tremaine had heard all about it. Her notoriously single granddaughter galivanting with a Westmoore would be big news to her. Isis would never live it down, and Willa Tremaine was not the type of woman to just let things go.

Perusing her closet, Isis scowled at her choices. She'd worn her pink day suit the last time she'd gone to brunch with her grandmother. A simple sundress wouldn't do for meeting with the great Willa Tremaine. She scowled, she didn't lack choices, but nothing that suited her mood this morning would be good enough. Her choice was complicated. She could be comfortable and further piss off the woman, or suck it up and play the role expected of her, minimizing the emotional damage her grandmother was about to rain down.

Fuck it! My grandmother is already pissed. I might as well complete the trifecta.

Isis grabbed her light blue jumper and pale pink pumps. She dressed it up with the pink pearl necklace and earring set her grandmother had given her last year for her birthday. She grabbed her purse and headed out the door.

"You look nice this morning," Ms. Mable said.

Isis smiled at her elderly neighbor. She was bent over to pick up a small package in front of her door. Isis went over to help the woman so she wouldn't throw her back out again.

"Thank you, just on my way to the Regency for brunch with my grandmother," Isis said.

"Well, I won't hold you up. If you could just place it on the coffee table."

Isis nodded and put the box where the woman asked before making her exit. Maybe her good deed wouldn't go unnoticed, and today wouldn't be so bad after all. Her hope was short-lived. First, Willa was alone at the brunch table when Isis arrived, tea and mimosas already on the table.

"You're late," Willa said. Her grandmother smiled as she gave her a kiss on each cheek. The smile didn't reach her eyes, and the chaste kisses were like an arctic wind across Isis' cheeks.

"I'm sorry, there was an accident on High," Isis said.

Isis wasn't actually late. Her grandmother had demanded she come earlier than their usual brunch hour. A fact that Isis was beginning to suspect was on purpose. Brunch wasn't typically a solo affair for them.

"You should have left earlier. You know how I despise waiting," Willa said.

Isis fought the urge to bite her cheek or show any other sign of agitation with the older woman. Willa had only gotten harder to deal with as the years went by without Isis getting married. The worse it got, the more Isis understood why her mother had fled to Europe to live the artist's life with her latest lover. Unfortunately, that left Isis to deal with her grandmother alone.

"I will keep that in mind," Isis said, taking her seat.

"You do that," Willa replied.

There was nothing Isis could say to that, so she poured herself a mimosa.

"How has your week been? Are you still enjoying your afternoon tennis sessions?"

Isis hoped to lead the conversation to something neutral, but Willa narrowed her eyes at her.

"Why did I have to hear from Barbie Fisher that you are seeing Bechet Cross?" she scolded.

Strike One.

"I am not seeing him. He went with me as a favor," Isis said.

"Don't lie to me, young lady," her grandmother said.

Strike Two.

"I'm not. I didn't have a date, and Jay couldn't step in. Mr. Cross overheard and offered to escort me. It was a one-time thing, and it won't be happening again."

Isis knew she shouldn't lie to her grandmother like that, but the alternative of telling the truth would open a whole other can of worms.

"And why not?" she asked.

"We don't get along." At least Isis wasn't entirely lying about that.

Strike Three.

"Meaning you blew it. Your chance to settle down with one of the Westmoore family. An heir to the fortune," Willa huffed.

And there it is!

Isis downed the rest of her mimosa. She didn't need the extra alcohol loosening her tongue around her grandmother, but definitely needed to calm her nerves if she was going to keep up a convincing facade. Isis loved her dearly, but this one issue was turning into a major wedge between them.

"It wasn't like that," Isis said.

"I'm disappointed in you, child. Whatever foolishness you did, I need you to undo it," she said.

Isis did her best not to roll her eyes.

Focus, Isis. We can handle this. Just like when grandmother found out about Richard.

Her gut turned at the memory of that showdown. Then again, as she realized that this was just the warm-up. It was only a matter of time before her grandmother brought up Richard's engagement to Rachel. If she'd heard about Bechet, she'd surely heard about the engagement as well. Isis wasn't sure if it was her anger at her current situation or the alcohol, but words spilled out of her mouth before she could stop them.

"Bechet Cross is not some grand prize, grandmother. I have aspirations that don't include being someone else's arm candy. I need to make a name for myself, and being on a Westmoore's arm basically ensures I will be seen as nothing more than a trophy piece."

Willa reared back like Isis had physically slapped her. "There is nothing wrong with being seen as a trophy piece. I'm not saying you can't have a mind and ambitions. Just, why deal with all that stress when a man with his family connections can grease the wheels for you," she said.

"I don't want wheels greased unless it's my own grease," Isis said.

The words didn't really make sense, even to her, but that was what downing two mimosas on an empty stomach could do to a person.

"The only grease you got is between your legs, and it's high time you get that through your head. Hell, even that might not be enough anymore. You couldn't even hold on to Richard. Let Rachel Headley of all people slide right all up in the wheel you were greasing for months and steal it," Willa spat.

Fuck!

Isis downed her third mimosa and the waiter came by with a fresh pitcher and refilled her glass. She took a sip and nearly spat it back out. The fresh pitcher was noticeably lighter in color than the first and a quick glance at the waiter confirmed that this batch had purposefully been made stronger. Was it that obvious how shitty this conversation was going?

If Isis hadn't already felt something about the Richard and Rachel situation, her grandmother had hit the final nail in the coffin for Isis' ego. She could give two shits about Richard and Rachel, except for how it looked to others. She'd hoped it wouldn't reflect poorly on her as a person, but her grandmother had just confirmed all of her fears.

Willa could be mean, but she wasn't that creative with her comebacks. Her grandmother had heard something along those lines from someone else. Someone in her circle of powerful friends, and that meant Isis's name was being dragged through the mud. This brunch wasn't their usual meeting to catch up. This was her grandmother putting her on notice. The world was shitty, and Isis didn't even have the support of her own family.

The only support she seemed to have was the waitstaff who obviously thought more alcohol was exactly what she needed to get through this situation. What Isis really needed was something more than a few pieces of fruit. She was just about to signal the waiter to bring food when Barbie Fisher herself came waltzing into the room.

"You two started without me. I should be offended," she laughed, plopping down into the seat next to Isis.

Barbie and Isis' grandmother shared a look that Isis was too tipsy and angry to decipher at the moment. Worse, Isis lost her chance to politely leave as two more of her grandmother's friends joined them. Leaving her grandmother to chat with her best friend, perfectly fine. Leaving before the food arrived now that the whole brunch group arrived would only add more fuel to the rumors her grandmother had so casually thrown in her face. So instead, she reached for the pitcher of mimosas and settled in for the real brunch.

❖❖ ·· ·◆· ·❖❖

Bechet woke up to the sun burning his eyeballs out of his head. He had no idea how much he drank last night, but it had obviously been too much. Bechet frowned as he realized he wasn't home in his apartment, but in a hotel room, and he was still in his tux. He forced himself out of the overly soft bed and rubbed the grit out of his eyes.

He needed to get home and clean last night off of him before he could get on with his day. Bechet fixed his tux as best he could and wandered out of the room. Kevin was sitting at the kitchenette reading the newspaper.

"Morning, bro!" the man chuckled.

"Thanks for letting me crash last night. I was not at my best, and I apologize," Bechet said.

"No worries, bro. I promise not to hold it against you much."

Bechet shook his head. He really wasn't feeling being at Kevin's place. It wasn't a good look, not only from a business perspective but a personal one. He knew that Kevin would use this against him one day. That was just how the man worked. Nothing he did was out of simple goodwill. The man always had an agenda, often a self-serving one. Last night had really gotten to him if he had allowed himself to be caught up in one of Kevin's many webs. There was no way he could just chill with Kevin like this, even before getting to know Isis.

"Right, well. I guess I'll see you Monday to discuss business," Bechet said and hightailed it out of there before Kevin could keep him any longer.

Kevin kept a penthouse at the very top of K Hotel, so at least Bechet didn't have to worry about finding a way back to his car. He took the elevator down to the lobby and headed for the valet. As soon as he slid inside, his phone buzzed with a text from Dom.

D: I'll understand if you can't make our weekly game. You hit it pretty hard with Kevin last night.

Bechet texted back immediately.

B: Nah. I'll be there.

He was just about to toss his phone to the side when an idea struck him. With a devious smile, he scrolled through his recent contacts and dialed Isis' number. She didn't answer, which wasn't surprising, so he sent her a text.

B: I'm giving you one more chance. Be ready to go at 1pm. We're going out.

He was surprised, however, to see that she replied almost immediately

I: I already have plans

B: Cancel them.

I: Goodbye Bechet

He ran his hand over his face. He knew he should just let it go, let Isis go, but for whatever reason, that just didn't seem like an option for him. He drove home and took the time to rehydrate and get back to some semblance of himself before going to pick her up.

❖❖ ·◆· ❖❖

Isis was pissed that Bechet seemed to think she was at his beck and call. Especially after Saturday. If only spending time with Bechet wasn't infinitely more appealing than her actual plans. Not that she had any intention to go out with him again, even without the excuse of prior plans. Her grandmother sat chatting away with her friends about the mundane things society wives did, as if that whole shitshow hadn't just happened between them.

They were on their third pitcher of mimosas, and food had just been delivered when Isis received Bechet's last-minute invitation. If she were just a tad soberer, she would have ignored her phone completely. It was rude to check your phone at brunch, and Isis was already on thin ice with her grandmother. If there was any ice left to stand on between the two of them. Willa had made it clear she wouldn't tolerate Isis' aversion to the marriage market any longer.

Still, as she sat at the brunch table with her grandmother obliging her socialite duties, Isis couldn't help but keep checking her watch. It was just past noon. She'd been there for hours, but it seemed like days.

"Do you have somewhere you need to be?" Willa asked, annoyed.

Maybe she could use the texts as an excuse to leave, but that would only bring more questions. If she admitted it was Bechet on the other end, then her grandmother would get her hopes up, and that would only make the situation worse.

"Sorry, no," Isis said in a hushed tone before turning to Barbie and joining the droll small talk.

Stop checking your watch!

Isis didn't know why she was so anxious about not meeting up with Bechet that afternoon. She even caught herself debating if she should reconsider since brunch ended in time for her to still technically make the requested date. The choice was taken out of her hands. While waiting at the valet for her car, none other than Bechet pulled up.

"Get in, or we'll be late," he said.

Isis glared at him, squinting her eyes just enough to obscure the tempting view of his chiseled features and dazzling grin.

"And if I refuse?" she asked.

"Then I will get out and ensure your grandmother gets an eyeful of us together," he said and nodded behind her. Isis turned to see her grandmother was thankfully engrossed in conversation with her friend Mindy, and not currently looking in their direction.

Isis sighed and got into the car. "How did you know I was here?"

Bechet turned a brilliant smile her way. "You have a lovely neighbor, Mable, who was thrilled to inform me that you were having brunch at this establishment with your grandmother.

Normally, Isis didn't mind her sweet but nosy elderly neighbor, and it wasn't like Isis did much to feed the woman's need for gossip. Still, she really wanted to give Ms. Mable a good talking to about telling strangers her business.

"Just drive around the block a few times and drop me back at the Regency," She grumbled, and he shook his head before turning onto the freeway in the opposite direction of the hotel.

He didn't say anything more as they pulled up to the Mulberry Hill Community Center. Isis had no idea what they were doing there, but she didn't have to wonder long. Once they were inside, he handed her a towel and a water bottle before heading to the basketball court, where a group of men and teens were waiting on him, including his cousin Dominic. They started up a game, and periodically Bechet would jog over to get a drink or towel off. Isis rolled her eyes at him, and he just winked before returning to his game. Since Isis didn't have her own car, she was forced to wait until he was finished.

Well, not exactly forced, she could have called a cab, but she was captivated by the sweat glistening on his bare chest. The man could easily star in any of her mental fantasies as long as they stayed just that, fantasy. No matter how attractive Bechet Cross was, Isis just couldn't put herself out there with him again. Bechet didn't say a word to her until he was done playing, and of course, the first thing out of his mouth was a cliché flirt.

"Like what you see?" He spread his arms, flexing his taut pectorals and washboard abs for her perusal. Isis let her gaze slide over his flesh like she wished she could do with her tongue before shaking her head and remembering that he was an asshole she wasn't supposed to be associating with.

"Can we go now? I have more important things to do," Isis grumbled and stormed away to his car.

"Oh, you mean like the important things I canceled to be your date?" he said.

"You mean the date you inserted yourself into," she replied.

Bechet sighed but didn't say anything more. Isis pulled out her phone and checked emails until he stopped the car.

"Let's go," he said and got out of the car. Isis sighed and got out. At least she could walk home from there, but instead, he took her arm and led her to the elevators.

"Seriously?"

Bechet's chest heaved with another heavy sigh.

The elevator doors opened to the penthouse, and he guided Isis into his bachelor pad. It was a lot homier than she expected. No sparse modern décor for him. He was all rich wood and heavy throws. More mountain chic than big-city bachelor. Seeing how easily he moved through his space gave her a better sense of who he was, or at least who he was trying to portray.

"What am I doing here?" Isis asked.

"We need to talk, and I need to shower." He shrugged before disappearing into the bedroom.

Isis heard the shower come on a few seconds later and knew she should leave but didn't. Instead, she perched on the couch for a minute before its lush comfort enveloped her, and she nearly fell asleep wrapped in its softness and the many scents of Bechet Cross. Not willing to let herself get caught napping, she forced herself from the couch and over to the wall of photographs on the other side of the room.

It didn't take Isis long to realize it was a family tree of sorts. On one side was the Westmoore family, and on the other was the legacy of the Cross. On the Westmoore side, each photograph depicted different eras and stages of the barbershop's growth and notoriety. From the opening to the present, each male owner had his picture taken in front of the storefront window holding a pair of scissors in one hand and the keys to the place in another, ending with one of Bechet standing with the rest of the Westmoores, next to Dominic. The Cross' on the other hand, told an entirely different tale. In logging jumpers and flannel, burly white men stood amongst vast logs with massive axes and saws in hand. Generation after generation until it showed the first Cross Logging offices. It was similar to the Westmoore journey, only Bechet didn't look as proud in his photo as all the men before him.

Isis was so focused on pondering why she hadn't noticed the water had stopped running, nor that Bechet was standing so close to her. Just watching.

"My family has a grand legacy to uphold, but that doesn't mean we couldn't do with a little change," he said, startling her.

Isis jumped back only to collide with him. His arms came around her, causing the towel he'd been holding to fall from his waist. His manhood pressed into her back, and on instinct, she spun around to push herself away only to pause as her hands came in contact with his muscled pecs. Her breath caught for a moment, but Isis didn't dare look anywhere but straight ahead.

She attempted to make space between them, but Bechet held her firmly against him.

"Look at me, Isis," he said, his voice demanding but strained.

She shook her head but didn't make any further attempt to distance her body from his. Isis felt him growing thick and hot through her jumper. She shifted slightly, the fabric stroking him in lieu of her hands which she kept firmly on his chest. With a curse, he let her go and grabbed his towel. Bechet didn't cover up but turned his back to Isis, giving her the full view of his taut backside as he strolled into his bedroom and closed the door.

Isis resisted the urge to follow and demand he take her like her body desperately wanted. Instead, she moved her shaky limbs over to the couch and sank into its welcome embrace.

What the hell is my problem? Why can't I just cut my losses and leave?

She knew the answer to her questions, but that didn't mean she was any less perplexed.

Bechet Cross just could not be the man for her. It was that simple. Even if her libido insisted otherwise. Bechet came out a few minutes later, fully dressed and smelling like heaven again.

"You think we can have that talk now?"

"I think I can manage," Isis lied.

She was still in a sexually aroused trance and in no condition to have a serious discussion with the man who put her in it. Still, it was now or never, so she sat up straighter and focused on the pigeon taking a shit on the rail of his balcony, instead of the gorgeous man sitting across from her. He reached out and took her hand in his.

"I believe we may have a few crossed signals."

Bechet was amazed Isis had stuck around instead of bailing the moment he left her alone to take a shower. Even more amazed that she was still sitting here looking deliciously turned on after he'd embarrassed himself just a few minutes earlier. Every logical part of his brain told him to just let her go. She was too cautious, too self-righteous, too stunningly beautiful for him to ever think that anything between them could end in anything short of a disaster. Yet here they were on his couch. The sexual tension was heavy in the air as he held her hand and gazed into the never-ending depths of her chocolate eyes.

"Crossed signals is putting it lightly," Isis finally spoke.

"We had a great time on our lunch date and dinner later. I thought we were on the same page as far as what we said we wanted."

"We were. I mean, I thought we were. I did a horrible job of explaining myself the other night, and I just. Do you know how frustrating it is trying to be more than people's expectations of you? I'm sorry I took it out on you, and I should have done my research before agreeing to whatever this was."

"I know exactly how frustrating it can be. So, you don't want to continue this?"

"Why? Do you? We have already proved that we don't fit each other's needs."

Bechet scooted closer and pulled her onto his lap. Her bottom fit snugly against him as he ran his palms along her belly. She bit her lip, eyes fluttering shut, back arching into his touch. He slid his hand up further to cup her breast, eliciting the sexiest sound he'd ever heard escape from her lips. It was half whimper, half moan, but the best part was that it vaguely sounded like his name.

"Sounds like we fit just fine," Bechet said before capturing her lips with his. He had every intention of showing her just how well they fit when his phone began to ring. He would ignore it, except the chiming bell's tone was for his favorite little cousin.

He positioned Isis under him so she couldn't make an escape before reaching to answer his phone.

"Bechet, you promised you would be here," Alicia whined.

"Sorry! I got caught up with a last-minute negotiation," he said.

He had totally lost track of time, but it had more to do with the gorgeous woman beneath him than anything work-related, as his answer implied.

"Well, hurry up and get here. Mother has at least fifteen women here, conveniently single and your age, waiting for your arrival," she said, and he cursed.

"I'll be there shortly," he said and cut off the phone.

Bechet turned his attention back to Isis, kissing her into writhing desperation before sitting up and pulling them both off the couch.

"Before you write me off for good, I demand a return on my investment in this not relationship."

"You are unbelievable," Isis said.

"I just need you to keep the husband hunters away during my baby cousin's party. I mean, you are dressed for the occasion and are covered in my cologne. It's an easy sell."

Bechet wasn't trying to be crass, but he also didn't want to further ruin things by showing any attachment, when that was obviously the last thing she wanted. No attachment was what they had agreed on after all. When her back went ramrod straight and her once gooey lustful eyes turned hard and cool as ice, Bechet knew he'd made yet another miscalculation.

"I'm not asking you to pretend you are my girlfriend. Just don't make your contempt of me so obvious is all I'm hoping for."

The rooftop gardens at the Mulberry Art and Culture Museum were most debutantes' dream event space. Isis had been there for events several times before but never for a teen coming out party.

"Finally!" a beautiful young woman said, rushing to give Bechet a hug.

"I told you I would be here," he said just as she noticed Isis. The teenager gave Isis a quick once over before frowning.

"You brought a date?" she asked, and he chuckled.

"An associate. I brought an associate," He clarified.

The young girl gave Isis another once over before rolling her eyes and taking off back to her guests.

"You couldn't have even said friends?" she asked, hating that she felt some type of way about his cautious introduction.

Bechet smirked and leaned close to whisper in her ear. "I try not to lie to family. This is not a date, and you are not my friend," he said before walking off and leaving Isis standing at the entrance to the party on her own.

Isis scanned the room and only saw maybe three people she recognized. None of them was anyone she would gladly converse with on any occasion. One was a work associate, the other being his wife, and the third was an acquaintance from her old debutante days, who was obviously there for a chance to snag the attention of one of the elusive Westmoore bachelors.

She was just about to suck it up and head over to her coworker and his wife when she was intercepted by none other than Kevin.

"You look like you could use a drink," Kevin said, handing her a glass of punch.

As much as Isis wanted to throw the drink in his face, she didn't want to make a scene, so she accepted the glass but didn't take a sip. She forced a smile and nodded, hoping he would take the hint and get lost, but Kevin just smiled back. Isis was taken slightly off guard by his genuine smile, it held zero snark, and his eyes didn't spark with mischief. It seemed even Kevin had some sense of decorum.

Who knew?

"Thank you," Isis said and took a tiny polite sip before making a move to find where Bechet had abandoned her, but Kevin stopped her again.

"I think it's high time we cleared the air between us, Isis," he said.

Isis wasn't interested in clearing the air with him. They literally had no connection aside from a few shared high school friends and now Bechet.

"There is nothing in the air to clear. It is obvious that we just aren't meant to be friends. I am good with that," Isis said.

Kevin frowned and took her hand in his.

He brought it to his lips and brushed a soft kiss across her knuckles. Isis quickly pulled her hand away and glared at Kevin. She was unnerved to see the glimmer of shock in his eyes that she wasn't swooning over his efforts to be charming. His eyes turned dark in a dangerous way, and Isis took a step back right into Bechet's arms.

"Kevin, what brings you out to Alicia's party? I thought kid events weren't your thing," Bechet said, an unfriendly edge to his voice.

Kevin looked between Bechet and Isis, a sick glint in his eyes.

"Coming-out parties always get the debutantes in the mood. I'm sure you know what I mean," Kevin winked at Bechet.

Isis felt sick to her stomach at the reminder of what Jay told her about Bechet's relationship with Kevin just that morning.

"I don't know what you mean, and I hope you didn't sneak in as my plus one. Isis is my guest," Bechet said, neutral enough. Still, the tension in his grasp, combined with the devious grin on Kevin's face, told Isis there was much more going on than just simple posturing between the two of them.

"Always going for the haggard ones. To think I learned anything from you is a wonder. Let me know if it's anything like fucking a corpse," Kevin said and walked away before either of them could say anything.

"What an asshole! I'm sorry, I wouldn't have brought you if I'd known he was here," Bechet said.

Isis turned and glared at Bechet, but he was too busy glaring at Kevin's back. "It seems Kevin is a closer friend than you led me to believe."

Bechet turned to her with a confused expression, "I told you there's nothing but a business relationship there."

"I don't know what is going on between the two of you, but I will not sit here and be humiliated," she hissed in his ear.

"You are so quick to the wrong judgment. Let me make sure he leaves and then we can talk about this habit of yours," Bechet said with a huff and walked away from her again.

Kevin and Bechet's exchange had not gone unnoticed. Neither had her little tiff with Bechet. Isis smiled awkwardly before making her escape. She certainly wasn't going to go begging Bechet for a ride home after that hideous display.

Bechet wanted nothing more than to wring Kevin's neck. The man was a nuisance. Business deal or not, Bechet would no longer be associated with anyone that classless. He tracked down Kevin to kick him out of the party, but his aunt was already on it.

"I think it would be best if you exited quietly before you ruin any more of my daughter's event," she said.

Kevin smirked before downing his glass of punch and dropping it on the ground at her feet. That was the final straw. Bechet hadn't intended to make a scene at his cousin's party, but somebody needed to put Kevin in his place, and that person was Bechet. He grabbed Kevin by the collar and lifted the smaller man off the ground until they were eye level.

"You will not disrespect my family or me ever again," he dropped Kevin back to his feet while his cousins grabbed the man by the arms.

"You will regret this. Our deal is through," Kevin said in a low menacing voice.

"I don't need you or your shit deal," Bechet replied, getting in the man's face.

A wave of malice washed over Bechet making the hair on his arms stand on in. For a brief moment, Bechet thought he saw wisps of black smoke surround Kevin's black soulless pupils. He took a step back just as security arrived to escort Kevin out. As soon as Kevin was gone, Bechet turned an apologetic look to his aunt.

"I'm sorry for disrupting the event. It wasn't my intention."

She grabbed his hand and patted it gently. "It's not a party if no one gets thrown out," she laughed.

Bechet smiled, before going in search of Isis. She had been a little brusque with him, but that didn't mean he had to be rude to her. She was his guest after all, and despite her penchant for judging him harshly, he still liked having her by his side. When she wasn't where he had left her, he assumed she'd gone to the bathroom. In his brief experience with her, anytime she got upset she would go there to reset and come back out as if nothing had been wrong. So, he waited a few minutes before sending her a text.

B: I'm sorry Kevin has once again turned our time together sour.

He waited a few minutes with no response before texting her again.

B: I am also sorry for being rude. I just wanted to make sure Kevin wouldn't be an issue for the rest of the evening so we could enjoy ourselves.

When there was still no answer, he sent Alicia to the bathroom to look for her.

"Sorry, Bechet. She wasn't in there. Maybe she's wandering the gardens. I saw someone about her height entering the hedge maze," Alicia said before rejoining her party.

After searching the whole garden twice, Isis was nowhere to be found. He was just about to call her and ask where she'd disappeared to when he was cornered by his cousin Dom.

"So, you and Jay's girl?"

"Jay's girl?" he asked, a sinking feeling outrageously close to jealousy filling his gut.

Dom smirked and shook his head. "Not like that. Jay and Isis are close friends, just friends. I'm just saying you have already decided to make a go of it with her, so be careful. The Queen of Ice has felled men much greater than you. I'd hate for there to be any tension at the shop if things don't work out."

Bechet frowned. "You saying you'd fire Jay if things go south with Isis and me? That doesn't make any sense."

"You're right. It doesn't. I meant you'd be getting bowl cuts from grandpa instead of down at the shop with me. Isis has thick walls, but she's a nice lady. I know your reputation, cousin. Just like I know hers. Don't be that guy here, is all I'm saying."

Running a hand over his face, Bechet let his cousin's words sink in. "Either way, have you seen her? She disappeared after what happened with Kevin."

Dom nodded his head toward the main entrance. "Yeah, she left a while ago. If I were you, I'd go after her sooner rather than later."

Dom didn't have to tell Bechet twice.

Traffic had been thankfully light, given it was a Sunday evening. In no time, she'd gone back to the Regency for her car and then straight home. That meant she had plenty of time to stew while showering off the scent of Bechet's cologne. Then she ignored Bechet's texts and calls as she ordered a pizza, changed into her most comfortable pair of sweats, and lazed on her couch to vent her frustrations with a violent video game.

"Stupid men." *Kick.* "Asshole creeps." *Punch.* "Yeah, rip his head off!" *Fatality!*

The gory scene on the screen was probably not the healthiest coping mechanism, but when nursing a broken heart, there was no better way.

Broken heart? What the fuck?

Isis realized she shouldn't have this issue and had seriously lost her mind. The lines she'd sworn not to cross kept getting blurred and redrawn in her mind. She should have stayed to hear Bechet out but with the scene they had made, in the social circle of her grandmother's dreams. No way could Isis have stuck around like a lovesick puppy, waiting for Bechet. Especially when it would only fan the flames of the rumors threatening to burn down everything she'd built in the last few years. So she'd bailed and focused on the fact Bechet had lied about his relationship with Kevin. Another unnecessary lie from the man who otherwise seemed her perfect match. The doorbell rang interrupting her intruding thoughts.

"Pizza, right on time."

Only instead of her usual pizza delivery person, Bechet was at the door with her food in hand and a smirk on his face.

"Mind if I join you for dinner?" he asked.

Isis scowled at him before snatching her pizza and attempting to slam the door in his face.

Bechet slid his foot in the way, and the door bounced back open, allowing him to come inside. He closed the door behind him and followed her to the couch. Isis tossed him an extra controller before restarting her game and grabbing a slice. He'd been calling and texting her nonstop for the last hour, then made the trip to her place. The least she could do was hear him out while kicking the crap out of him in her favorite game. Beating the computer and randoms online was fine, but beating Bechet in the flesh? Even better.

"I never pegged you for a pizza scarfing gamer," he said after Isis kicked his butt in the fighting game.

"Funny, I pegged you for an asshole the moment I met you," Isis said, and he had the nerve to laugh.

"So, I'm an asshole for abiding by our mutual agreement," he said.

"Look, I didn't have all the facts before agreeing to it," Isis said.

"How does that make me the asshole again?" he asked.

"How does it not? You misled me and left me on my own at your cousin's party."

"I stepped away for one moment. How was I supposed to know Kevin was there and would accost you? I've also been one hundred percent clear on everything I felt was pertinent information. I don't know what more you want from me, Isis. I feel like anything I say you will turn into something it isn't, so what's the point?"

Isis sighed. He was mostly right. She would probably turn anything he said into something else, and she couldn't help it. He'd already let her down enough that she had a hard time feeling like she could trust him. What else was he hiding from her? The real question, why did it even matter to her if this wasn't a real relationship?

"We have nothing to do with each other, and our only commonalities are trivial. Why are we even still talking about this? I'm not some object or toy to pass around with your friends, nor am I some bet to be won."

Bechet shook his head. "What are you even talking about right now? I would never do what you are implying," he said.

"Really because putting me into demeaning situations is totally the actions of a man who would," Isis said, standing.

"If you are talking about me bringing you to my weekly basketball hang, you had plenty of opportunities to leave. What does it say about you that you went along with these so-called demeaning situations?" he said, standing as well.

He was mere inches from her, and his cologne wafted around them, turning whatever argument she could have had to meaningless dribble in her head. She held her breath to keep from inhaling more of his mind-melting scent.

"Can you take a step back?" she asked.

He smirked at her and moved just a hair closer.

"Why?" he asked.

Isis tried to take a step back but tripped over her own feet. Instinctively, she reached out to steady herself but only proceeded to pull him down with her. They landed in a heap on the floor, and he raised up slightly, shaking his head at her.

"You alright?" he asked.

She nodded, unable to trust her mouth to form proper words at this point.

"If I didn't know any better, I would think you were trying to seduce me," he muttered before rolling off and helping her to her feet.

"Seduce you? As if," Isis scoffed and made a show of shivering as if disgusted by the thought.

Bechet pulled her flush against his body and kissed her. Not roughly but a gentle brush of his lips over hers. Isis melted into his embrace with a soft moan. He chuckled softly before kissing her again. This time he parted her lips with his tongue, and she kissed him back. His arms tightened around her as the kiss became more passionate. Clothes went flying as Isis guided him back to the couch.

There was no more thinking, just sex-starved bodies out of control. They were naked. He was on top of her. His hard cock bobbed in the space between them. Isis gripped him, thick and hot in her palm, stroking him, feeling every vein along the length of him. She guided the tip of him along the curve of her hips and thighs. So very close and yet still too far from the one place she knew they were desperate to touch. Bechet took a deep breath and pushed away from her once more.

"I don't have a condom. I didn't expect..."

Isis fell back onto the couch with a groan. She was truly losing her mind. Despite their bodies' desperation, it seemed even the universe was signaling that it wasn't meant to be. Nudging her and reminding Isis that she wasn't being overly cautious when it came to Bechet. So instead of offering up her personal stash, she shoved her arousal out of her brain and dug deep to find the outrage she felt earlier over the whole exchange with Kevin.

"Get the fuck out, Bechet."

"Isis."

At his confused expression, she pulled herself off the couch, picked up his clothes, and threw them in his face. "I said get the fuck out!"

His confusion was replaced with anger before Bechet grabbed his clothes and got dressed. At the last moment, he reached for her one last time, placing a chaste kiss on her forehead.

"Goodnight, Queen of Ice," he muttered before walking out of the front door.

Her blood ran cold. Bechet's words were just the affirmation she needed that kicking him out was for the best. She didn't need that kind of distraction in her life. She grabbed her sweats and slid them back on before getting comfortable on her couch again. This time with a pint of her favorite ice cream.

As much as she knew his leaving was a good thing, it didn't stop the tears or the sharp needle prick pain in her chest as her mind replayed the night's events. As she looked at the last week in hindsight, she sank further and further into sadness and quilt. How could she have fallen for someone like Bechet? Not only that, how had she managed to fall so fast. It had only been a week, and he'd managed to get further beyond her walls than any man ever had.

CHAPTER FIVE

The view from his apartment just wasn't doing it for Bechet that morning. The more he stood on his balcony, the more he thought about Isis. The first night they met when she'd captivated him from afar. He should have heeded her warning then. He should have let her enjoy her time alone, but no, he'd pursued her. He'd gone after her despite every twist, turn, and hard stop she'd thrown his way. Until now. Now he would give her what she'd demanded of him from the very beginning.

He went back inside and poured a second cup of coffee before sitting down at his computer. He sent Margo and the rest of the team an email telling them to drop everything from the K Hotel deal and to focus solely on the Corinthian. Bechet didn't regret ending his association with Kevin. It was long overdue, but the loss of such a huge deal was something he was going to need some time to recover from.

He wasn't at all surprised when his phone began to buzz, showing Margo's number.

"Morning, Margo," Bechet wasn't exactly a morning person, but even he knew his tone was a little gruffer because of what happened with Isis.

"You sound like shit. What happened that made you change your mind so abruptly?"

Bechet sat back in his chair, trying to decide if he wanted to open up to Margo about Isis. Margo had been there to help him with damage control after Rachel. As happy as she may be that Bechet was done with Kevin and this deal with K Hotel, she would not be happy that he had endangered the success of his business over relationship issues again. Even if the circumstances were different.

"A little too much face time with Kevin. Anyway, I hope there isn't too much lost with all of this. We had barely begun the needed ramp up, and the extra workers for the K Hotel deal can be easily shifted to the Corinthian bid," Bechet said.

"Of course, it shouldn't be an issue at all. Good thing you hadn't designed anything yet; otherwise, I'd be kicking your ass right now. I am happy to shift our focus to Corinthian, but there is one more thing I wanted to discuss with you," Margo said.

"Yeah, what's that?"

"Scarlett is back. She's doing some business in Sowell City that she's hinted could be beneficial to Cross Furniture," Margo said.

Bechet laughed. Scarlett King was not only Margo's cousin but one of his first investors. Despite her party-girl reputation, she had a knack for investing in startups and helping them grow to their full potential. He was honored that she had signed on when Cross Furniture was little more than an idea.

"Just hinted? That isn't Scarlett's style," He laughed.

"She's been really cryptic about what's she's up to lately. It's a bit troublesome, but you asked if there were any new business leads, so there you have it. You two are friends. Maybe if you reached out, she would be more open to conversation," Margo said.

Bechet scowled at that. He may be friendly with Scarlett, but he wouldn't exactly call her a friend. The potential had been there. At least until his mother tried to push a romantic relationship between the two of them. That had ended in disaster as neither of them was interested in settling down, especially not then. To top it off, Scarlett had eventually been banned from all Cross family events after she ruined one of Bechet's mother's rare chances at hosting a society-style party at the Cross Estate.

"Hunter is in Sowell City frequently these days. Maybe he can track down what she's been up to and get a clearer picture of things," Bechet offered.

He wasn't exactly in the mood to be social nor was he quite ready to head home. It would feel too much like a defeat at this point. Coming home without the K Hotel deal and no real solid leads on something bigger or better for the company. It would only further prove to his father and older brother that Bechet just wasn't worthy of the Cross legacy.

Bechet's thoughts were interrupted by a series of rapid clicks. "Are you texting her right now?"

"It's called multitasking. Get with the times, Chet," Margo laughed.

"If we weren't friends, I would end this call right now. This isn't how you do business, Margo," he chastised.

"I'm helping you out here so you can just be annoyed a second longer," she replied.

The edge in Margo's voice put Bechet on edge himself. "Is something wrong? You said Scarlett has been cagey lately? Do you think she's in trouble?"

"I'm not sure," Margo admitted after a second.

After coming out, Margo's entire family had disowned her. Everyone except Scarlett. Bechet wasn't sure how Margo would handle it if Scarlett wasn't okay.

"Call Hunter, and try not to worry too much. I'm sure Scarlett is alright."

"No need. Scarlett has requested a lunch," Margo sighed.

"When and where?"

"Today, Café Yarrow."

Bechet checked his calendar. He knew there was no conflict now that the K Hotel deal was over, but he checked anyway. He wasn't sure he was up for dealing with the whirlwind that was Scarlett King, but if she had business for him, how could he justify ignoring her request.

"Fine, set it up. I'll see you both there," Bechet said.

"Great! We'll talk business, and then we can tag team her to see what's really going on," Margo said.

"Yeah, let's do that."

Bechet didn't even try to hide his lack of enthusiasm this time, and Margo knew just how to shift the conversation, so it stabbed him right in the gut. "So, since the Kevin deal is done, are you going to head back to Edgewood?"

Bechet took another sip of his coffee and sighed.

"Yeah, the few plans I had this month are obviously canceled. Unless something comes up by Friday, I'll be heading home," Bechet said.

"Well, don't sound so sad about it. I promise things will work out. See you at lunch," Margo said before hanging up.

Bechet stared at his phone for a few minutes. His focus should be on business but all he could think about was Isis. Yeah, they'd both said some things that they regretted. Well, he regretted calling her the Queen of Ice. He wasn't sure Isis regretted a single thing she said to him, he just wished he had a better idea of why they just couldn't seem to get it right. So instead of texting her, instead of calling and groveling he set his phone down and looked up the latest news on his computer. The mayoral scandal was still front-page news and had even started getting the attention of some major news outlets. Apparently, after digging further into the mistress's claims, there were things that just weren't adding up. Bechet sighed and clicked away from the gossip, and went back to work. He didn't care about politics anyway, and with Isis not talking to him, there was no need for him to get into it now.

Three days and no word from Bechet. Not that she expected anything after how she'd thrown him out, but that hadn't stopped her from checking her phone every five minutes anyway. At least at work, she was slightly better at ignoring the fact that things were done between them.

The mayor's scandal was big news. So much so that it was hard not to have it be a major part of her daily conversations, be it with fellow politicians–making bets on the outcome and what it would mean for their own career aspirations–or with her constituents–who wanted more details and reassurances that the buck-passing wouldn't land in her lap.

"You should take a break. You are visibly wilting," Hector said, handing her a bottle of water.

Isis snatched the bottle and gulped it down before putting the empty plastic in a nearby recycling bin. She usually carried her own refillable bottle, but she'd forgotten it on the counter this morning. Along with her sanity, apparently. She was holding on by a string, not because of Bechet but because of everything. There were only so many subtle and sometimes blatant aggressions any person could take in so few hours.

Checking her watch, Isis sighed. "It's almost one. Let's break for lunch and meet back here at three to finish this neighborhood," she said.

"A two-hour lunch? You sure you're okay?"

"You would rather I say we grab a snack and keep going?"

Hector adamantly shook his head and started to back away. "No, no. See you at 3!"

He jogged off before Isis could change her mind and call him back. She pulled out her phone and texted the rest of her team about the extended lunch break before ordering to go from Café Yarrow. With the long lunch, she could have enjoyed her food there, but she wasn't in the mood to sit alone in public. A quick rideshare later, and she was trudging up the stairs of the Café, ignoring the looks of the trendy hipsters who frequented the place. She knew she looked like shit, glistening with sweat in her campaign shirt and jeans. The soles of her shoes flapped with each step. She'd swap pairs when she got back to her office. For now, she followed the heavenly smells of vegan soul food to the pick-up counter.

"Ms. Hale! Your order is almost ready," the hostess greeted her.

Isis nodded and stood to the side, out of the way of the other customers. Her gaze drifted over the small dining area. It was late for the lunch crowd but still busy with the younger college-aged crowd who had more flexible schedules. She was just about to turn her attention to her phone and the plethora of emails waiting for her when she spotted him.

Bechet was in a booth along the far wall, and he wasn't alone. A cute brunette sat next to him, not across but right next to him. Her head turned into the crook of his neck. Her hand rested gently on his chest as she did so. She hadn't expected to run into Bechet again, especially not here. Not at the place she had introduced him to, and with another woman no less.

For a moment, Isis forgot about her food. She turned to head for the exit, but the hostess called her name.

"Ms. Hale, your order," she said.

Isis snatched the bag of food from the hostess and took off down the stairs. "Thank you," she called belatedly over her shoulder. It wouldn't make up for how rude she had been, but all Isis cared about at that moment was getting far away from Bechet and his date. If she'd needed any reason to justify her decision to leave Bechet Cross alone, she'd definitely just gotten it.

Bechet forced a casual smile as Margo casually whispered to him that Isis was there in the restaurant.

"I've come here a few times hoping to rub shoulders with her. Do you think you could introduce us?" Margo asked.

Bechet cleared his throat.

"No, we had a mutually beneficial reason to go to one event together. We aren't friends," he said.

Margo scowled and checked her phone again. "I can't believe Scarlett stood us up," she muttered.

Becher took her moment of distraction to look up. Hoping to catch a glimpse of Isis to see if she was feeling half as shitty as he was about how things ended between them. He didn't get the chance. She had already disappeared. Instead, Scarlett was headed their way.

"Look who decided to grace us with her presence," Bechet said, getting up to greet Scarlett.

She laughed and flipped her long brunette hair over her shoulder, a feature she shared with Margo, but the only one. Whereas Margo was slim and sleek in appearance, Scarlett had carefully cultivated curves and a flashy attention-seeking demeanor.

"Oh, Chet, you know I love to make an entrance," she said.

"Yes, we do but an hour, Scarlett. That's pushing it even for you," Margo snapped.

Scarlett slid into the booth and sighed. "I was actually on time, but they don't allow dogs, so I took Matty for a doggy spa day," she said.

Bechet sighed and settled back into the booth with Margo.

"How is Matty doing, by the way?"

"He's adjusting to the collegiate life. I know you don't really care about Matty, so let's get down to business, shall we?"

Bechet relaxed as he saw Scarlett visibly shift from her party-girl persona into business mode. Maybe this lunch wasn't going to be a waste after all.

Isis closed herself into her tiny office, exhausted and frustrated. Her appetite was gone, and her takeout from Yarrow was still wrapped in its eco-friendly packaging on her desk. She should go home, but she'd rather be at work and not thinking about Bechet. The asshole hadn't bothered to even call to let her know that their deal was done. Not that he had no reason to, because she had effectively ended things, but out of courtesy. She closed her eyes for a second, taking a few calming breaths, and when she opened them again, she nearly jumped out of her chair.

"What the fuck are you doing here? Who the hell let you in here?"

Kevin smirked, standing in front of her closed door. He raised his hands as if to say that he wasn't there to do any harm, but she knew better. Kevin was the definition of harm.

"I see you still aren't ready to talk," he said.

"There is nothing to talk about. Get out!"

"Will you just hear me out, and then I'll go. I promise," Kevin said.

Isis glanced at the sole window in her office. The blinds were closed, no one could see in, and it was far too noisy outside for anyone to hear what was being said inside her office. She felt trapped and uncomfortable. She was already standing, so she pushed her desk chair in front of her body and additional shield against Kevin in case he tried to do something to her again.

Kevin noticed her movements, and his usual smug smile slid into place.

"I always knew you hated me but never once did I think that hatred was tied to fear. Are you really that afraid of me, Isis?"

"Only a fool wouldn't be," she spat.

Kevin shrugged.

"Truer words were never spoken, alas I'm not here to hurt you. I am actually here to help," he said.

Isis watched intently as he reached into his briefcase and pulled out a thick manilla envelope.

"What is that?" she asked.

"Everything you need to make the ultimate boss move," he said, placing the envelope on her desk.

Isis didn't move to touch it.

"I don't want your money," she said.

"It's not money, although if you need campaign contributions, you know where to find me," he said, his eyes traveling over her body.

She shivered. "I don't care what's in that envelope. I don't want anything from you."

"Not even if I'm literally handing you the keys to the city? If you don't accept my help, another will, and I can't promise you'll like what the outcome of that will be," he said.

"You don't help people. You use them. I'm one of the few politicians left in town that isn't in your pocket, so fuck no. I don't want shit you have to offer," she said.

Kevin's smile dropped, his expression turning dark.

"We've never been friends, Isis, but we've also never truly been enemies. I'd like to keep it that way," he said.

"Why?" Isis couldn't help her own curiosity.

"Because you're the last sliver of light in my life," he said.

Isis cringed. "I'm not anything in your life. Get out, Kevin."

"You are, and I need you to stay that way. I need you to prove to me that the darkness isn't all-consuming," Kevin said.

His tone was almost pleading, and Isis didn't know what was creeping her out more. Kevin showing any level of vulnerability, proving that there was something human beneath all the shit, or the fact he thought she had any importance to him and his life.

"Leave now," she repeated.

Kevin looked down at the floor, and the temperature in the room rose at least ten degrees. When Kevin looked up, his pupils were so wide there was almost no white showing. He looked inhuman, possessed. His mouth curved into a sneer, and for a moment, Isis swore there was a shimmering black aura around his body. He took a step closer, and she backed against the wall. Her body trembling with fear.

"I could make you like me. With just a touch, I could make you mine," he growled, closing the space between them.

Isis was pinned in place. Caught between her fear and anger. She reached deep, focusing on the stronger of the two emotions.

"I'll never be yours. I'll never be anything like you," she snapped back.

"There she is, the ice to my fire. It's fascinating. You are so weak in comparison, but manage to be so incredibly formidable."

"Fuck you," Isis said.

Kevin took a step back and closed his eyes. She watched as he fought whatever the hell had come over him, and when he opened his eyes, the brown pits of despair were back, a second glimpse of the vulnerable Kevin that had taken her by surprise just moments before. Only now she knew for sure it was only a ruse. The darkness was still there, had always been there.

"I'm leaving now. It normally goes without saying, but since it's you, I'll be very clear. What happened just now never happened. I wasn't here. We never spoke. I'll not interfere with you again," he said.

Isis sagged with relief for a moment before a sickening thought came over her. "What about Bechet and the Westmoores?"

Kevin shook his head. "I'll not interfere with you again," he repeated before leaving her office.

As soon as he was gone, Isis sank into her chair. The tension in the room released slowly like a balloon with a pinprick. She eyed the envelope that was left on her desk with a scowl before pushing it into the trash with the edge of her pen. She didn't dare touch it with her bare hands. Then she pulled out her phone and scheduled an emergency appointment with her new therapist. Whatever fever dream she'd just had needed to be addressed.

Hector appeared in the doorway of her office. "I thought when you closed your door, you were taking a nap, but clearly that was not the case," he said.

Isis sighed. "What do you want?"

"Well, I was going to ask if you wanted to get a drink with us tonight, but from the looks of things, you just need to go home."

Isis rolled her eyes. Us meant Hector and the three other volunteers that Isis attempted to be friendly with. Hector was right. She was not up for drinking tonight. Still, the idea of going home and being alone with her thoughts after the shit day she had, wasn't high on Isis's to-do list.

"Drinks sound nice as long as it's someplace low-key. It's not exactly a good look for me to be out partying right now," Isis said.

Hector laughed. "Don't worry. I have the perfect place in mind," he said.

The perfect place turned out to be a party at his family's dance studio. Apparently, there was a competition-level dance team that practiced there, and they'd recently won a major competition. Isis was surprised at how much fun she was actually able to have, even though she did avoid dancing. She was good enough for posh soirees and ballroom dancing at a charity event, but humble enough in her abilities to stick to the sidelines as the professional dancers did their thing.

Isis was just beginning to relax and forget about everything troubling her when everyone's phones began to buzz. Well, maybe not everyone's, just hers and her favorite volunteers since they were the only ones with notifications set for breaking news about politics.

Isis had just decided to ignore it, letting the buzzing fade in her pocket, but Hector came rushing over.

"Oh my god! Isis! This is huge! A catastrophe but fucking huge!"

She scowled. "Whatever it is can wait until tomorrow. I promise," she said.

Hector shook his head. "No, Isis, it can't. We need to put Plan Isis for Mayor into the works ASAP!"

"What?!"

Hector held out his phone, and Isis nearly collapsed to the floor. The breaking news was literally the entire political world crumbling to the ground. Leaving only one major player and a few low-level politicians unscathed, including herself. A recording of a private conversation between the mayor and a few other key politicians had been leaked, revealing not only the truth behind the mayor's affair but also the financial fraud and illegal deals for campaign contributions. Suddenly Kevin's words about handing Isis the keys to the city made much more sense. She had passed on Kevin's deal, but she was pretty sure she knew who had taken him up on it.

Kevin had been right about one thing. She was not happy about it at all.

"Fuck," she cursed.

CHAPTER SIX

"**Y**ou look like hell."

Bechet turned away from the view of the mountains outside his home office window and glared at his brother. He'd been home a month already. At first, the small deals with Scarlett's latest business projects had kept him bus in Sowell City. Not enough time for him to sit and dwell on Isis and the failure of the K Hotel deal.

"You know knocking is common courtesy."

Braxton Cross shook his head and plopped down in the oversized leather chair opposite Bechet.

"Look, I know that deal with Kevin the douche fell through, but I think the Corinthian deal is better suited to our brand anyway. No use moping about it. Unless that's not what you are moping about," he said.

Bechet sighed and tugged at his beard.

"I knew it! Dom told me you had some lady trouble in the city."

"Don't you have some furniture to make?"

Bechet wasn't going to discuss women with his older brother. The man had run his way through most of the single women dumb enough not to heed the warnings of others about the wild Cross brothers.

Braxton shrugged and pulled out his phone. "I need you to make this deal work, so I have material and funds to make my art."

"You have plenty to start already."

"Sure, sure. Anyway, Isis Hale is hot as fuck. You think she's into hairy men?"

Bechet stormed across the room and grabbed Braxton by his shirt. He was just about to tear his brother a new one when their mother walked in, hands on her slim waist and a disapproving scowl that sent Bechet back to his childhood days.

"Bechet Anderson Cross!"

He put his brother down and dusted off his shoulders with a smile.

"Apologies, mother. I was just showing Braxton a new jujitsu move."

Melinda Westmoore-Cross shook her head before entering the room.

"Braxton, go back to your workshop. Bechet and I need to have a talk."

"Yes, Mother," Braxton gave their mother a quick hug before scooting out of the room.

Bechet sighed before escorting his mother to the couch his brother had just vacated.

"So, tell me about Ms. Hale. Your aunt was so excited to tell me all about you making a scene at your cousin's party."

Bechet groaned. He should have known his aunt would tell his mother about that, but it had honestly been the last thing on his mind. All he could think about, besides how he would dig himself out of the hole he dug with Isis, was finding a new contract for the company. Scarlett's business was much appreciated and gave him a reason to take a break from Mulberry, do some work closer to home. Still, it wasn't going to be enough to make up for what was lost with the K Hotel deal. Honestly, Bechet was surprised his mother had waited an entire month to bring it up with him.

"We hung out a few times. It's nothing to gossip about."

"Really? I don't recall you ever being possessive over a woman. Especially to the point of putting her above business."

"I wouldn't call it possessive. In fact, I was the perfect gentleman, like you taught me. I couldn't let my guest or myself be so disrespected."

"I get that, but I can tell there is more to the story. You don't usually flaunt your relationships in the public eye, and rumor has it you could barely keep your hands off the girl."

"Look, we may have had a connection, but it's over now. I'm back home, refocused on what's important."

His mother scoffed at that. "So focused you've been moping around the estate, staring out of windows and muttering to yourself about difficult women? Honey, I raised you. I know when you are stewing and when your feelings are hurt."

"It's not like that, really," Bechet said.

He wasn't sure if he was trying to convince himself or his mother. Either way, it didn't seem like it was working. She gave him a soft smile and patted his cheek.

"You're a grown man, and it's your life. I just hate to see you so worked up. If you really care about this woman, I think you should go back and try to make things work with her. If your father and I could do it, so can you."

With that, she stood and left his office. Bechet didn't have time to ponder his mother's words as his phone began to ring. He jumped on the chance for a distraction, and it was well worth it.

"I've got news! How fast can you get back to Mulberry?" Margo sang through the line.

Bechet smiled, knowing that at least one of his problems was about to be solved.

Isis surveyed the people gathered in Dominic Westmoore's living room with a smile. This party was the culmination of all her hard work. She was finally being accepted on her own terms and reputation. With Bechet out of the equation, she wasn't the least bit distracted from her goals.

Things seemed to be looking up for Isis in terms of her career.

A major scandal had hit the city, and here she was, a prime candidate for the next Mayor of Mulberry. The current mayor got caught up in a scandal that not only ruined his career but those of most of who would typically be considered his replacements. Meaning a young progressive junior politician such as herself was getting a once-in-a-lifetime shot at making a significant career jump. It was an opportunity that Isis just couldn't pass up.

Her reputation was squeaky clean, and with the Westmoores' endorsement, she was in a prime position to win. As long as she stayed above reproach. Her smile faltered as her gaze traveled back to over the guests in attendance. The subtle shift of the group revealed Bechet, looking as smug and delicious as ever in a black suit, no tie. The top button was undone, exposing just enough of his golden chest to send Isis' heart speeding into dangerous territory.

Worse, on his arm a gorgeous brunette in a stunning red dress. It drew attention but was cut in a way that was more elegant than flashy. They looked the perfect couple. Isis could almost feel the stares as she clenched her champagne glass tighter than was necessary. She tore her gaze away and muttered a half excuse about needing the ladies' room. After setting her drink on a nearby table, she walked in the direction of the restroom but then made a beeline for the door.

"So, you were going to leave without saying hello," Bechet said, catching her arm.

Isis looked around for any excuse to remove herself from his presence but could find none. Especially with so many eyes on them. It was her fault for coming to Dominic's house party, and if he hadn't agreed to endorse her campaign, she probably never would have. If she had known Bechet would return now looking hot as hell and with another woman on his arm, the same woman she had spotted him with at Café Yarrow, she undoubtedly would have declined the invitation.

"Shouldn't you be more worried about your date?" she asked, and he chuckled.

"Margo? She's an old friend," he said.

Isis scowled at him. "A friend?"

She hated the sharp kick to her gut; this woman was a friend, while she had only been an acquaintance to him. Isis tried to move away from him, but Bechet guided her away from the door and further into his cousin's house. He stopped in the hallway just past the restrooms, not quite secluded but far enough away to avoid being seen or heard.

"Yes, an old friend. One who wanted to meet the woman who drove me to distraction the last few months," Bechet said.

The reminder of him basically ghosting her was almost enough to switch Isis' brain back to proper function.

"Please go back to your date," Isis sighed as Bechet pressed her into the wall. Caging her in, surrounding her with his too familiar heat.

"Did seeing me with her make you jealous?" he asked, nuzzling her neck.

"No," she breathed. Bechet began to kiss down her neck, brushing his lips along her collarbone.

"I believe we've already had a discussion about lying," he laughed.

"You're the liar here," she replied.

"I have never lied to you, Isis. Would never." Bechet looked her in the eyes. It was clear he was trying to make a point.

"You try not to lie to family. I'm not your family."

"Not yet," he said, taking her mouth before she could say anything more.

Isis hated how her body betrayed her but loved every hot zinging sensation he gave her. Without realizing it, Bechet had guided Isis further down the hall and into an empty room, locking the door behind them. The only light came through the large windows that overlooked the skyline. The coincidence was not lost on Isis. All major events between them seemed to happen above ten floors. She faced him, doing her best to seem completely focused and not at all affected.

"Mr. Cross, this is not funny."

He turned her back around to face the stunning view from Dom's penthouse and unzipped the back of her dress, pressing soft kisses along each inch of her newly exposed spine. She arched her back.

"Bechet," she murmured as her dress slipped free from her torso.

"Have I ever told you how sexy it is when you say my name like that?" he growled before turning her back around.

His shirt was wide open, exposing tanned skin dusted with dark brown hair. She'd known him to be mostly clean-shaven, but apparently, he'd embraced his mountain man heritage in his absence from Mulberry's societal life. He dipped his head to capture her bare breast in his mouth.

Isis moaned and sank into his hold as he worked her up. His hands slid into her panties to touch her core while he suckled, and all thought outside of riding him until release ceased to exist at that moment. Isis wanted him inside her so badly, but it seemed he had other plans. Bechet released her breast and slid down to his knees. He grabbed her thighs, lifting her legs over his shoulders and pressing her back against the cool glass. She watched in the mirror on the other wall. Their profiles in shadow against the bright city lights. Like a strange beast as she pressed her hands against the glass.

Bechet buried his face between her legs. Alternating fingers and tongue in a tantalizing dance over and within her dripping flesh. He tongued her until she was writhing and begging for release. Then he pulled her from the glass holding her weight as if it were nothing. He carried her to the bed.

"Keep your eyes on the view, baby," he gasped before he slid up her body and entered her with one quick thrust. He sheathed himself completely inside of her, and Isis came apart in a multicolored haze of pleasure. His mouth covered hers, muffling screams before he began to move and take his own pleasure. Her muscles milked him as waves of pleasure continued to wash over her with each thrust. Bechet slammed into Isis one last time and stilled, spilling into her.

Bechet continued to kiss her until they were both coming down from the high of their mutual orgasm as a soft knock on the door brought them back to reality.

"Shit, shit, shit!" Isis cursed, looking for an escape route.

Bechet pulled out, a huge grin on his face before fixing his pants and making his way over to the door.

"Just stay on the bed. I'll get rid of them," he said.

Isis did her best to pull on her dress and calm her nerves before he could open the door. The few years of quick-change skills from her short-lived pageant days were really coming in handy. She managed to get decent before Bechet could go forward with his plan. She slid through the crack in the door with a sheepish grin.

"Sorry, I just needed a little break from the party." Isis made the lame excuse as both Dom and his female companion gave her knowing looks.

At least the party seemed to be over. Only a few were still lingering as Isis headed straight for the front door. She didn't have to turn around to know that Bechet was hot on her trail. When they reached the elevator, she put as much space as she could between them.

"I must be out of my fucking mind," she cursed as the doors slid closed.

Bechet hustled her against the wall and kissed her. "If you are, then so am I. I'm not finished with you, Ms. Hale. Not by a long shot."

"What about your date?"

"I told you, it's not like that. Besides, I assumed you would have your own arm candy present and wanted a buffer for any jealousy that brought."

Isis rolled her eyes at that. "And what do you care? I'm the Queen of Ice, remember?"

Bechet sighed and brushed a finger along her cheek. "Honey, there is nothing icy about you. I'm sorry I called you that. I was upset, and I lashed out like a silly child. You know just how to get under my skin, Isis."

She shrugged and turned her face into his hand, pressing a soft kiss to his palm. "I should never have let this happen. It's stupid and crazy."

"And perfect."

The elevator slowed, and Isis slid from Bechet's grasp.

"I just need some time," she said before taking off.

This time Bechet didn't follow, and Isis hated the disappointment she felt that he hadn't.

One night, that was all the time Bechet could allow her. He'd already spent too much time away as it was. He'd come back to Mulberry two months ago to finalize the deal with Corinthian. Yet, he'd stayed away at first. He'd tried to give her space. Tried to see if his feelings would dissipate with time. They hadn't, and both of them had been busy with their respective goals. He hadn't wanted to be a distraction to her. Had waited to see if she would move on., if she had moved on. She hadn't, and neither had he.

If the Corinthian deal hadn't hit so many snags, courtesy of Kevin, he would have made his move sooner. Bechet had lost three months of pining for a woman who seemed intent on pushing him away. He put his hand in his pocket, touching the small velvet wrapped box that held the bracelet he'd foolishly purchased, because the stones reminded him of her radiant smile.

Isis Hale had worked her way, not just under his skin but into his heart. He'd tried to ignore it. Tried to be reasonable, but nothing was reasonable about the way he felt. The bracelet had been an impulse buy. Carrying it now, he had no idea what his plans were with it. He'd only meant to test the waters with her. See if she was open to starting things up again. Then he'd seen her last night, and all caution went out the window. He hadn't expected for his dick to take over, not saying he minded. He would only regret it if last night was the only time.

Bechet was ruined for other women now, and he knew for a fact that no one would ever hold a candle to Isis Hale. Making up his mind, he took the short walk to her place in stride. The smell of sweet pastries and bacon reached his nose before he got to her door. His mouth instantly watered at the tantalizing aroma and the image of him licking sweet maple syrup from her skin.

Shaking his head, he readjusted himself in his slacks before knocking.

Isis was just finished topping the waffles with dulce de leche and whipped cream when there was a knock at her door. It was too early for anyone she knew to just stop by. Isis was tempted not to open the door, but she sighed and put her fork down when the knock sounded again. Her heart nearly stopped when she peeked through the peephole to see none other than Bechet Cross standing in the doorway.

After their run-in at his cousin's house, she hoped he would get the hint. Apparently not, if he was showing up at her door.

"Go home, Mr. Cross," Isis called through the door.

"I just want to talk," he replied.

She didn't believe that for a second. From past experience, talking with Bechet Cross meant doing anything but. "So, start talking."

"You really want me to say what I need to say out here? Where anyone can overhear?"

Isis groaned. It was bad enough he was at her door this early in the morning. The last thing she needed was for her neighbors to hear all of her business, especially with her mayoral campaign underway. She reluctantly opened the door.

"There is always this thing called a phone, but since you have already proven not to understand the concept of distance communication..."

She stepped aside and let him in. As soon as the door closed, he pulled her into his arms and kissed her.

"I'm sorry about last night. Not the sex, but for not contacting you sooner."

Isis appreciated the apology, but it didn't lessen her embarrassment over the situation. "Is that all?"

She pushed out of his grip and went back over to her plate of food. She tried not to pay attention as his hungry gaze followed her every move.

"I came to ask you for a second chance."

Isis snorted and shoved a mouthful of waffles into her face to keep from spewing the first thing that came to her mind at him. She chewed slowly, taking the time to sort out her thoughts and feelings.

"Despite my lack of better judgment last night, I don't deal with taken men," Isis said, and he laughed.

"Who says I am taken by anyone but you?"

"I'm sure Ms. Buchanan is wondering where you are at this very moment."

Bechet rolled his eyes.

"I'm sure she is at home snuggling her girlfriend right now. Much like I'd hoped we would be doing last night. I told you before, she is a friend, and I mean it. I'm not attracted to her in the least."

Isis shoved another bite of food into her mouth. Chewing angrily because—while the logical side of her brain was fighting tooth and nail to not give in—her poor, desperate little heart was slowly winning the battle.

"You left for three months without a single word. What makes you think I want anything to do with you?"

"If last night was any indication..."

"It wasn't."

Bechet crossed the room, plucking the fork from her hand. He turned her to face him. "Are you sure?" he asked.

"No, what I want is to drag you into my room and ride you like a rodeo girl, but I can't do that."

Being this close to him, heat flooded her body, and her mind ceased to function as arousal pooled between her legs. One thing Isis could never deny was that the sexual chemistry between them was off the charts but was that enough to justify putting herself out there?

"And why not?" he asked.

"Because you belong with someone else. Someone content to be just a pretty fixture on your arm."

"Wrong, Ms. Hale. I belong with you and you alone. I never wanted a participation trophy. I want the real deal Olympic gold, and that, for me, is you," he said and swept her off her feet, before carrying her to the bedroom.

Isis knew she should stop but couldn't help herself. She wanted him, so she took him. All of him until neither of them could function.

Isis woke up later that afternoon snuggled tight against his rock-hard body as Bechet continued snoring like a lumberjack. She slipped out of bed and slid on a robe before heading to the kitchen to clean up breakfast and figure something out for a late lunch.

The time to herself gave Isis space to think and to clear her head away from the man who was everything she wanted and everything she didn't need all at once. Trying for once to be absolutely logical about the situation, Isis began a pros and cons list regarding Bechet Cross.

Pros. He obviously checked off all her boxes in terms of attractiveness and professional ambition. He was well connected, so she didn't have to worry about him using her for her connections. The sex was definitely not an issue for them either. They got along well enough on their first date, so she knew the connection between them wasn't purely physical.

The cons. His connection to that creep, Kevin. The fact he continued to find ways of pushing all her buttons. The fact that associating with him meant others might not take her seriously in her own right.

"You look tense. Did I not work out all the kinks?"

Bechet's voice cut into her musings. He was standing on the other side of the kitchen island in nothing but his boxers and a mischievous grin. Isis nodded for him to sit at her small table while she brought over plates of her thrown-together pasta.

"We haven't even begun to scratch the surface of my kinks, but that's beside the point. Let's eat, and then we can have a serious conversation."

Bechet nodded and took a bite of pasta. He moaned a deep satisfied groan. "Marry me," he said.

"Not a chance," Isis laughed.

They didn't speak again until both plates were clear, and he pulled her into his lap.

"If everything you cook tastes this great, I might be serious," he laughed.

"You really aren't, and I have no time for your games," Isis said, standing.

She took their plates over to the sink before going into her room to shower. She didn't protest when he joined her. "Before you get any ideas about shower sex, I'm just going to tell you upfront. I am absolutely insane for wanting to give you a second chance, but I need to clear a few things up."

Bechet smiled and crowded her body against the wall of the shower. His thick cock pressed against her stomach.

"Ask me anything."

He began to trail kisses along her neck, and Isis tilted her head to give him better access. Her hips pressed closer to him.

"Your relationship with Kevin."

Bechet froze and pulled away from her. His expression was one of disgust.

"First, I never want to hear any other man's name while we are intimate, especially not his. Second, I am no longer associated with that disrespectful piece of shit."

"First, I told you not to start anything because we needed to talk. Second, glad to know." Isis reached for him, and he took her into his arms. Standing under the spray of her showerhead, they held each other for a moment.

"I have a feeling your distrust of anything Kevin related is a deeper story. You don't have to tell me the details if it makes you uncomfortable but if or when you are ready to talk about it. I'm here," Bechet said.

Tears welled in Isis' eyes. That was the last thing she expected him to say. Most men would have demanded she tell them the story or not cared at all.

"To be honest I haven't told anyone, not even Jay. I don't know when I'll be ready but thank you for offering your support."

Bechet wiped a tear from her cheek.

"Is there anything else bugging you, my love."

Isis bit her lip. His calling her love had her heart jumping for joy, and she wasn't sure she could adequately continue this discussion with a clear head. It was obvious that she was a lost cause and that her heart had made up its mind. Bechet Cross was it. She stood on her tiptoes to kiss him before grabbing her loofah to finish washing up.

Their conversation was tabled until they were out of the shower and back in her room.

"Don't say things you don't mean. I have enough people blowing smoke up my ass, and I don't need it from you too. Also, I need you to consider my feelings and reputation before doing stupid things like chasing me half-naked through a party. I don't want you using your connections to help me with things unless I ask, nor would I ever assume any favors just because we happen to be dating..."

Bechet cut her rambling off with another kiss. "I've never met a more infuriatingly stubborn woman in my life, and that includes my mother. Yet, I find myself madly in love with you. Anything you ask of me, Isis, I am all in if it means you are by my side."

Now Isis really did swoon before she caught herself. "As long as you never call me the Queen of Ice ever again. I think I'll allow it."

"I promise never to repeat those words and as an added apology..." Bechet grabbed his pants from the floor and dug in the pocket before pulling out a jewelry box.

Isis frowned. She may be prepared to date him, but if he seriously proposed right then... She hoped he wouldn't.

"Bechet," she began but stopped when he opened the box to reveal a lovely silver bracelet set with a rainbow of different colored crystals.

"I'm not foolish enough to ask you to marry me yet, but when I saw this, I knew I had to get it for you. So please accept this gift as the first of many from your new man."

Isis laughed.

"My man? Really?"

"What, you prefer boo, bae, boyfriend?"

Isis secured the bracelet around her wrist and pulled him into her embrace.

"We'll discuss labels later. Right now, I want you in my bed, Mr. Cross."

Bechet smiled.

"Deal."

EPILOGUE

"I It's my absolute pleasure to introduce to you, Mr. and Mrs. Cross!"

Isis squeezed Bechet's hand tight as they entered the large reception hall. Friends and family filled the tables surrounding the dance floor, and there were only a few dry eyes in the bunch as they entered the space as man and wife.

Bechet guided her to the dancefloor, pulling her into his arms just as the song they'd chosen for their first dance began to play. Not the live band they had originally booked, but a recording of them playing it live. There had been a scheduling snafu after a sudden change in venue. The band had recorded the song live for them as an apology.

At the moment, though, Bechet could care less if it was the Barney song on repeat. All that mattered was Isis in her gorgeous white princess gown, eyes glittering with happy tears.

"We really did it. We managed to keep our sanity to make it to this day," she said.

Bechet rested his forehead against hers and pressed a gentle kiss to the tip of her nose, careful not to smudge her makeup.

"Yes, we did, even if only just barely," he chuckled.

They swayed to the music, the crowd watching them intently, the flash of the wedding photographer's camera going off every few seconds. No one would approach them during their dance. Isis had insisted that the tradition of pinning money on her gown and his suit wasn't one she wanted to keep. Bechet was sure she was worried she might get stabbed by a few of the jealous debutantes she'd been forced to invite by her family. Bechet agreed for his own reasons.

A few of the reclusive Cross relatives had come out of the woodwork to attend his wedding. Most notably, his Aunt Mirna, who was rumored to be a practicing witch. He didn't want to risk her trying some spell on them. Be it good or bad. One could never tell with Mirna. So anyone wanting to bestow money on the couple would have to be satisfied with putting it in the envelopes provided and dropping it on the gift table.

The song ended, and Bechet didn't want to let her go. In fact, he suddenly didn't care at all about the rest of the reception. All he wanted was to get her home and consummate the vows they'd said a few hours before.

Hell, he should have consummated them on the long-ass drive to their backup reception venue, but Isis had been too worried about looking disheveled when they arrived.

His wife, so image-conscious. Not that he could blame her. As the Mayor of Mulberry, she had every reason to be concerned with her appearance and reputation.

"Have I told you how proud I am to be your husband?"

Isis smiled up at him. "Only about twelve times in the car," she laughed and headed to the table at the front of the room.

He joined her at the table, and the wedding planner signaled for the caterers to start serving dinner. Then the Toasts would start. Dominic was in the middle of his speech when the doors to the reception hall burst open. Baron's wife Christine stumbled inside, draped in a K Hotel robe and little else.

"How dare you try to keep me out!" Christine yelled.

The near-silent filled with whispers as those who had no idea who Christine was began to speculate if she was there for Bechet.

"Who let that bitch in here?!" Aunt Mirna screeched over the murmur.

Bechet shot Isis an apologetic look, but she just squeezed his hand and smiled as if nothing out of the ordinary was happening. She had thankfully been spared from any previous introduction to his older brother's wife. Baron had moved Christine off the Cross estate before their first visit. The first step in getting rid of the wretched woman for good. How she'd even known the reception venue and how she'd gotten past security in such a state was a mystery.

Bechet watched in horror as the Cross clan began to rally, surrounding Christine, ready to fight if necessary. The wedding planner was desperately trying to get the Cross' back to their seats while Isis' security team stepped in to handle Christine, who was still throwing a tantrum about being excluded from Bechet's wedding.

"Baron! Baron! How could you let them do this to me!"

In all of this, Baron sat at the end of the wedding party table, sipping whiskey and not moving a muscle to help deal with his troublesome wife.

Bechet glared at Baron. It didn't matter, though. It was clear Baron had shut down. His eyes were unfocused as he stared straight ahead. Dom, however, continued on with his speech undeterred.

"It was fun watching Bechet and Isis fumble their way into love. I can only wish them both the best as they continue to grow into life together,"

"You can't do this! I'm still a Cross! I'm supposed to be here!" she wailed as they finally were able to drag her from the room.

Technically she was right about still being a Cross. Baron had filed for divorce a few months ago. A fact Bechet had heard from his cousin Elias, who was handling the divorce for

Baron. Even if they hadn't been splitting up, Christine had never been on Bechet's wedding list. She'd been a bitch to Bechet even before Baron knocked her up and was forced to marry her. Her behavior after that was all added fuel to his dislike for the woman.

"To Bechet and Isis!" Dom finished his toast.

Bechet turned his attention back to his cousin and best man. Dom had managed to get through his toast without faltering even despite the madness. A pillar of calm in the chaos. Bechet tipped his glass toward Dom before turning to Isis, who sat stiffly by his side. Ever the politician, she looked totally calm and happy on the outside, but Bechet knew better. She should be relaxed and happy, but their wedding had been anything but stress-free.

First, their original venue had flooded two days before the ceremony. Finding a last-minute venue that was classy enough for both Willa Tremaine and Melinda Westmore-Cross had been taxing, to say the least.

So while they had their big church wedding in Mulberry, the reception had been moved outside of town. The hour-long trek wasn't ideal in the least but had provided an extra layer of security against crashers.

Well, all but Christine. That had obviously been the last straw for her.

"I'm sorry my family is such a shit show," Bechet whispered in her ear.

Isis downed her champagne, and he poured her another glass. "It's fine. You warned me this might happen. Honestly, it could be worse," she shrugged.

It was not fine, and Bechet was sure that this whole incident would be top of the list of things discussed in their couples counseling session when they got back from their honeymoon.

Jay, the gentleman of honor, stood and started his own toast. His salmon tux, the same color as the rest of the bridal party. That had been another argument with the families. Jay was Isis' best friend, he rightfully deserved the role, but that hadn't stopped Isis' grandmother from trying her hardest to have Isis choose a woman from the family as her maid of honor.

Braxton gave his toast next. Bechet braced for some embarrassing childhood memories, maybe some uncouth teasing about the bear shifter sighting he had as a kid, but thankfully Braxton seemed to get the hint that the usual Cross Brother shenanigans weren't welcome in this space. His toast, while obviously stolen from a movie, still left tears in people's eyes.

Bechet had wanted to catch Braxton, to thank him for not being a shit brother like Baron, but of course, Braxton disappeared as soon as he got the chance. Shaking his head, Bechet decided it was best to focus on his new wife. His new family. His brothers and their drama didn't matter to him anymore. All that mattered was his Queen, Isis.

He found Isis chatting with her grandmother Willa and headed in her direction. Isis looked up as he approached, her eyes shining with happiness. Despite the earlier chaos she was still happy and that made him smile.

"Mind if I steal my wife away, Mrs. Tremaine?"

"We're family now, Bechet. You may call me Willa, and no, please enjoy," Willa smiled up at him.

Isis gave her grandmother a quick hug before dragging Bechet to the dancefloor. Once she was firmly in his arms she rested her head on his shoulder.

"Thank you for rescuing me. She was trying to get me to commit to spending our first holidays with my family," she sighed.

Bechet chuckled. "So I had perfect timing for once."

"Yes, you did. Now give me a twirl and let's get out of here."

"Anxious to start our honeymoon or trying to leave before any more chaos erupts?"

Isis looked up at Bechet and bit her lip. He saw the answer in her eyes so he spun her once before they headed toward the door.

Stella Williams

Stella Williams is a Blogger and USA TODAY Bestselling Paranormal Romance & Urban Fantasy Author, who lives in Washington State. She has a degree in Anthropology from The University of California, Santa Cruz. Stella prides herself in using her studies to create diverse worlds and characters for her novels. You can find more about Stella Williams on her website: www.stellawilliamsauthor.com

ALSO BY STELLA WILLIAMS

Sowell Gate Universe
Wild Cross Family

Felling Bechet

Yarding Braxton

Branding Baron

Reclaiming Hunter
Monsters & Mayhem

Peak
Unforgettable Contemporary

Unforgettable Valentine

Maura's Men Universe
Bloodlines

His Soul To Keep

To Catch Akellah
Secret of Ceres

Ferocious

Dauntless

Earnest

Zenith
Langsmith Shifters

Coy Wolf

A Night Divine

Bird of Prey
Maura's Men

Xander's Claim

Claude's Conquest

Shane's Redemption

www.ingramcontent.com/pod-product-compliance
Lightning Source LLC
Chambersburg PA
CBHW030635190726
48286CB00008B/2527